The Understudy's seco waiting to trip her. Sh running toward him, leaping over him at the last moment. She spun and landed a roundhouse kick against his chest as he stood up.

This brawler was tougher than her last takedown. He kept his feet firmly planted. He didn't deflect the blow, he absorbed it. He punched a meaty fist at her, but she spun into the smoke and disappeared from his view. She sidestepped, and the man predictably moved in a straight line after her. She went for another kick, but halted. Her mission wasn't to take everyone down. She needed evidence. She padded away deeper into the smoke.

The smoke dispersed to wisps and tendrils as the Understudy reached the edge of the smokescreen near the pier and boats. Two of the boats had already accelerated away out of range. The remaining had trouble. The motor raced. Either something was amiss, or the pilot had flooded the engine in a panic.

She raced toward the boat and stopped halfway. From the deck, multiple gun barrels pointed in her direction.

HOUR OF THE ROBOT

BY PAUL R. MCNAMEE

FOR CHRIS -
THX FOR THE ENCOURAGEMENT &
HEEP ALONG THE WAY!

Paul R. McNamee

MYSTIQUE PRESS

1. JOURNEY INTO EXILE

The ship sped through the sub-dimensions, hull shimmering in the space warp. Fins protruded from the aerodynamic bullet design of the spacecraft, a shape which allowed the spaceship to traverse both planetary atmospheres and the gulfs of outer space. The vessel passed a frozen dwarf planet, the farthest of nine in the solar system, and shot toward its distant sun.

The robot aided one of the crew to his feet. The alien shook his head and looked down at the empty glass chamber where he had spent the past three years in hibernation. Once he was sure of his footing, he straightened and stretched long, lithe arms toward the ceiling.

"Report," the alien said. He was humanoid, tall, and green-skinned. A lowering brow gave his eyes a dark, sunken appearance. He wore a blue flight suit with an alien emblem embroidered on the chest.

The robot crossed to the other side of the compartment. The robot had a humanoid form, a sleek red casing covered its frame except for openings to allow free movement at the joints. Black pinstripes ran down the center its arms, legs, and sides.

"We are approaching the orbit of the eighth planet of the system." Long robotic fingers pressed buttons along the edge of the cryogen pod. The glass door slid shut with a quiet hiss.

The revived alien, Vythor, nodded. After traveling countless distances through interstellar space, their objective was tantalizingly close. They would cross the orbital paths of a handful more planets as they headed toward the solar center of the system. Then they would be ready.

Vythor needed to be ready before then.

The robot moved to the next pod, analyzing readouts on the screens with its single electronic eye. It gave a moment's consideration to the data.

"Lieutenant Vythor, Captain Azomurn is reviving within acceptable parameters."

Vythor looked past Azomurn to the third hibernation bay, where another crewmember slumbered in the dreamless chill beneath ice-frosted glass. Her name was Krev. The robot initiated the revival sequence and then returned to the captain. As Vythor watched, the ice receded from the glass dome over Krev's capsule.

A groan turned Vythor's attention to their reviving captain. Azomurn sat up and fought away the confusion of hibernation. The captain was a hulking figure, wider and taller than Vythor.

Vythor wished the robot had not been so efficient. He had hoped his crewmates would not suffer. They should have continued to sleep deeply, lost in dreams. Vythor's attempt to alter the programming of his cryogen pod had failed. He should have woken first. He should have woken months before the others. Instead, the robot had been brought back online before Vythor. He cursed his luck.

Azomurn moved toward the pilot seat. Vythor needed to improvise quickly. He placed his hand on Azomurn's shoulder.

"Permit me. I have been awake longer."

Azomurn glowered, still in a post-hibernation fog. He was not one to idle long. As captain, he preferred a hands-on approach, but he accepted the logic of Vythor's suggestion and gave an irritated nod.

Vythor sat in the chair. Autopilot controlled the ship during hibernation. Once the crew were awake, it felt more reassuring to have someone at the helm. Computers and robots could do many things, but nothing could recreate instinct in a machine.

"Is the target what we expected?" Azomurn asked.

Vythor did not know if the question was meant for him or the robot. The robot was attending Krev, so Vythor answered over his shoulder. "Yes, but we haven't reached optimal scanning distance yet."

The ship still approached the eighth planet, and the distant sun appeared slightly larger. The planet was blue with five prominent rings. It was beautiful. Every planet Vythor had ever explored was unique. He wished their mission was a simple, peaceful survey. That would have been a more pleasant voyage than they were destined to endure.

They would not reach a safe distance for escape pod ejection until they had passed fourth, red planet. Vythor again wished for different circumstances, but it was not to be. Soon, Krev would be revived. He needed a distraction before he could begin.

With a glance, Vythor saw Azomurn watching the Krev's resuscitation. The cryogenic controls held the robot's attention. This was the only moment he would have.

Seizing his chance, Vythor slipped a small device from his pocket and attached it under the main console. The grey casing on the device shifted colors as the camouflage circuit engaged. The edges on the oblong device blurred, and it disappeared. It would deter all scans and could not be seen. Even touch would not discern the object from an imperfection in the console's surface.

If his crewmates had slumbered on, if the robot had not come online, the device would have been all that was needed. But Vythor could not risk the device being found. Though it was hidden, he knew there was a chance something would go wrong. He knew that all too well.

Vythor was onboard the vessel to ensure something went wrong.

A klaxon blared. Purple emergency lights bathed the ship's interior. A vibration progressed from the stern of the spaceship until the entire craft shook. Vythor felt a strange sensation of combined heat and chill permeate through his bones. His stomach roiled with momentary nausea.

Azomurn aided Krev to her feet. Like her male counterparts, she was bald. She stood slightly shorter than Azomurn and had a lithe body.

"What's happening?" Krev cried.

"Report!" demanded Azomurn.

Vythor saw a touch of disturbance in the captain's countenance. Had Azomurn felt the same sensations? Krev looked gray with nausea, but she had just come out of cryo-sleep. The simple act of standing could sometimes take inordinate effort.

Vythor spun his chair to face the captain. The other occupants of the ship appeared as if far down a corridor bathed in the purple hue of the alert lights.

"Warp imbalance!" Vythor said. He spun his chair back to the controls. The movement felt like it took a year. He stretched a hand and worked a combination of buttons and controls.

The vessel lurched to a stop.

The robot glided to the cockpit, scanned the outputs on the screens and started analysis. Azomurn supported Krev as they came forward, anxious for data.

"Was it pilot error?" Azomurn asked the robot, while glaring at Vythor. For a moment Vythor felt exposed, as though the captain had peered inside his mind and seen his duplicity. A chill ran along his spine.

The moment passed. Vythor shook off the thought. Azomurn couldn't have known Vythor's intention. If Azomurn had even the least suspicion, Vythor would never have set foot on the mission. He would have been imprisoned on Haephot. Why should the captain suspect him now?

Those of higher rank and influence had assembled the crew. Vythor and Azomurn would not have chosen one another as shipmates, but Krev had played peacemaker during the planning and training.

"No," the robot replied. "Nor are there faults in instrumentation. The warp drives will need to be examined."

The three aliens stared out the viewscreen. Against the darkness of space, the blue gas giant loomed large.

"I've woken up on better mornings," Krev said, a wry smile playing on her face. She appeared momentarily nauseated again, but the paleness of her skin flushed back to green.

Vythor quit the cockpit and strode to a bank of lockers on the wall.

"Where are you going?" Azomurn asked.

"To get a space suit," Vythor replied. He opened a locker. Red-orange environment suits hung above boots and helmets. "The engines need inspection."

"We will send the robot," the captain said.

"You can send the robot, too, you mean," Vythor said. He pulled on one leg of a suit. "I want to see those engines myself. I was in the chair, I feel responsible."

It was a weak excuse, but Vythor could not think of a better one. The tension distracted him. He fought down a panicked thought that his deception had failed. He imagined Azomurn toying with him, forcing him to damn himself further with every illicit action he would undertake.

Vythor paused and took a deep breath. He waited for the captain's official acceptance of his proposed action.

"Very well," Azomurn conceded. "Get out there and learn what happened."

Vythor's gloved hand shook as he opened the service hatch of the secondary warp drive. The secondary drive's function was to augment and balance the main drive. Without it, warping through subspace dimensions would be fraught with risk.

Across the stern of the spaceship, the robot inspected the main warp drive. Vythor had a few moments to act while the robot's attention was elsewhere. A hard-shelled tool case hung at his hip, the strap across his shoulder and chest. From a hidden compartment, he withdrew a device similar to the one he had placed in the cockpit. He secured it against the wall of the drive chamber. The device flickered into invisibility. Rather than override controls as the other did, this device would sabotage the warp drive directly.

The robot needed a problem to find. Vythor needed to create one. He studied a coupling that joined two rods, and reached for a wrench in his case.

"Report," Azomurn's voice crackled in Vythor's earpiece.

"Main warp drive is in perfect condition," the robot said.

Vythor felt a tinge of panic. With its inspection finished, the robot would come his way. He could not discretely use the wrench. In desperation, he grabbed at the coupling with his gloved hand. Vythor knew it was hopeless. He could not leverage the piece. His bare strength could not twist the coupling a machine had torqued into place.

He twisted his hand anyway. The coupling spun as easily as if it had been oiled and hand tightened.

Vythor felt delight and confusion in his moment of relief. He didn't understand how he had done it, but didn't have time to ponder.

"There is something amiss with the secondary drive, Captain." Vythor waved to the robot. "Come over here."

The robot fired boosters housed in the soles of its feet. It glided over to Vythor's side.

"There." Vythor pointed at a gap between the two rods in the drive engine.

"The coupling dislodged," the robot said.

"We must have come through something heavy while we were all sleeping," Vythor said. He hated lying, but he'd come so far with his deception it was second nature. "Meteoroids?"

"There are no dents or scoring marks on the hull," the robot said.

"An earlier warp imbalance?" Vythor suggested. "While we slept?"

"Any such emergency would have activated this unit," the robot said, referring to itself.

"What about the imbalance we just experienced?"

"That did not last long enough to have uncoupled these rods." The robot reached out its long metallic fingers and touched the coupling. Its single eye studied the arrangement of the rods and loose coupling.

"We can do analysis later." It was Krev's voice this time. "Robot—make the repair. Vythor, get back in here."

Stepping from the airlock, Vythor found Azomurn and Krev waiting. Vythor tried to attribute the suspicion on their faces to his own paranoia, but he knew they had discovered something. Perhaps he had not worn his lies and deceptions as casually as his cover required.

"What did you find?" Krev asked. It was a needless question.

"You heard me speaking to the robot," Vythor said. "A coupling came loose."

Krev and Azomurn exchanged glances. Krev nodded. "Interesting. We found this." Azomurn held out his hand. In his hand was the control device Vythor had planted on the control panel.

Vythor's expression remained calm. "Where?"

"On the control panel, in the cockpit," Krev said.

"I didn't see it."

"Neither did we," Krev said. "But as I watched you and the robot on the monitor, it appeared before my eyes."

Vythor feigned surprised. He took the device from Azomurn. He pretended he held an unfamiliar device, fingering the controls, until the unit disappeared on his hand.

"Camouflage circuit," Azomurn said. "Yet, we can see it."

Vythor stared at his hand. After a moment, he saw the device, too. He knew the camouflage circuit had not failed. He was not seeing it as it was, but as if through some other medium of sight—a different wavelength he did not know he could perceive. He blinked his eyes. The device was invisible again.

Azomurn grunted and grabbed the device from Vythor's open palm. Something cracked and crunched. The device re-appeared in Azomurn's hand; it had been crushed.

The captain looked incredulously at the shards in his hand. So did his crewmates.

"What is the meaning of this?" Azomurn asked. Vythor knew he wasn't referring to the attempted sabotage. Azomurn referred to the unexplained strength of his hand and fingers. Neither Vythor nor Krev had an answer.

The robot's mechanical voice came over the speakers.

"Captain?"

"Here," Azomurn responded.

"I believe it will be advisable to restrain Lieutenant Vythor."

"What? Why?" Krev asked. "Robot, what are you talking about?"

"The damage to the engine was recent and not accidental," the robot said. "I do not understand the method used, but only Vythor could have dislodged the coupling."

Azomurn scowled in anger. The muscles on his neck corded tight. He threw the pieces of the crushed device to the floor. "A device on the control panel. Damage to our warp drive. Care to explain yourself, Lieutenant?"

Vythor remained calm. The robot had only discovered the misleading damage Vythor had caused, not the second device. But if Azomurn or Krev informed the robot of what they had found, the robot would be certain to search for another device.

"I regret my action, but such actions are taken for the greater good." Vythor confessed.

Azomurn grunted without surprise.

"You are a separatist," Krev said. "An infiltrator." She snapped her mouth open and closed, at a loss for further words.

"And a saboteur," Azomurn said. "He threw us into warp imbalance."

"This vessel will not reach the third planet of this system." Vythor declared. "The separatist movement will not allow the machinations of the Haephotian Empire to conquer and exploit that world, or any other. We have knowledge and power to be used for peace, not conquest."

"We don't even know if it is worth conquering. That's why we're scouting." Krev laughed. "You have thrown your life away."

"Your report will never reach the home world," Vythor said.

"And if it doesn't?" Azomurn did not wait for an answer. "You are a fool, Vythor! The Haephotian Empire will not stop over the loss of one scout ship."

"Perhaps not," Vythor conceded. "But any invasion will be delayed. Delayed enough that pressure from dissenters might force change in the government. Delayed long enough for the planet—Earth, they call it?—to be warned and to prepare."

Vythor glared at his crewmates, defiance in his gaze. Azomurn's face blazed with anger. Krev seemed more disappointed than angry.

"Why not kill us in our sleep?" Krev asked.

"Exactly an example of brutality the Empire is too willing to engage in," Vythor said. "We hold ourselves to higher ideals. Our movement will not involve killing."

"Which is why your political movement remains impotent!" Azomurn snarled. Krev put a hand on his arm.

"What are we to do with him?"

"Good question," Azomurn said. "What indeed? There's no holding cell on this vessel."

"Put him back in hibernation," Krev suggested.

Azomurn shook his head. Vythor saw a glimmer of thought in Azomurn's eyes, but he couldn't interpret the captain's intention until it was too late. Azomurn bounded toward the armament locker. Vythor lunged, but Krev grabbed him around the midsection. He struggled and wrested free. He took a step and stopped short when Azomurn pointed a pistol at his chest.

"As captain of this ship, I can perform many duties," Azomurn said. "By your own confession, I hereby name you an enemy of the state. I name you a traitor, a saboteur, a mutineer, and a spy. I find you guilty. I sentence you to death. Sentence to be carried out immediately!"

There was a flash—but not from the energy weapon trained on Vythor. A cascade of colors shimmered as the main warp drive powered on. Vythor's device engaged. With the secondary drive sabotaged, the ship fell into another warp imbalance. There would be no overriding the engines from the cockpit.

The spaceship slipped sideways, spun haphazardly, all hope of navigation lost. The subspace tunnel stretched infinitely before them—an end never to be reached. Vythor bounced off the wall. He saw Krev and Azomurn lose their balance. They fell away from him.

Vythor thought of the robot, outside on the hull of the ship. Would it be able to reverse his sabotage? Could the robot hold on as the subspace warp imbalance contracted and expanded all around the ship?

Vythor jumped toward Azomurn. He had not expected to cross the distance in one move, but he slammed into the captain and drove him into the wall. Azomurn dropped the pistol. Vythor grasped one of Azomurn's wrists and pinned his arm against the wall. Azomurn's other hand slipped under Vythor's block and clutched his throat.

"What have you done?" Azomurn yelled. The rush of blood in Vythor's ears damped the captain's raised voice. The strangeness of the warp, combined with the damage being done to his windpipe, sent the room spinning in waves of color. Dark spots flecked in Vythor's vision.

Vythor strained against Azomurn's forearms. He broke free. Azomurn flew across the interior of the craft as though the artificial gravity had been turned off. He slammed into the wall, revealing a dent when his body crumpled to the floor. Vythor stared at his arms, disbelieving his strength. It was a wonder he hadn't heard Azomurn's bones break during the impact.

Other than a look of surprise, the captain seemed no worse for the wear.

Vythor inhaled a large ragged breath. He heard Krev trying to communicate with the robot, but there was too much interference in the signal.

Azomurn lunged, but Vythor had anticipated the attack. A solid blow to the captain's temple knocked Azomurn senseless to the floor.

From behind, Krev grabbed Vythor's torso, pinning his arms. She shuffled forward but Vythor struggled against her every step of the way. He saw the open hibernation chamber looming. Vythor swung his legs up, and his weight bent Krev over. He kicked the wall. Krev stumbled back, losing her footing and her grip.

There was only one way to escape the warp. One way to escape the ship. Vythor felt a moment of indecision. He locked eyes with Krev. He knew she saw his hesitation.

As he ran toward the rear of the ship, the walls blurred, but he attributed the sensation to the warp, not his speed. He entered codes in the keypad on the wall.

The door slid open.

Vythor leapt into the escape pod. Krev staggered to her feet. She closed the distance between them in a blink. Vythor managed to close the door. His fingers blurred as he programmed an override, even as Krev sought to enter the proper codes from outside. His codes engaged microseconds before she could countermand them.

Krev pounded at the door to the escape pod bay. Vythor could not hear her screaming, but her words were clear on her lips. He saw the door buckle under her blows. She should not have had the strength to damage the metal. Had the sub-warp distortion weakened the metal of the spaceship? Would the escape pod survive entering a planetary atmosphere?

Krev flipped on a comm channel.

"Coward!" Krev had seen his momentary hesitation. Understood it. She understood him too well. How had he taken his deception so far?

"So noble to leave us to our fate! Why don't you share it?" Krev banged her fist on the door. There might have been tears in her eyes. "Traitor! Coward!"

Vythor did not respond. He had nothing more to say. He engaged the controls. Rockets expelled the pod into the dark bosom of outer space.

The pod tumbled in the subspace warp-wake of the ship. The spaceship hurtled along its infinite voyage, trapped in the warp of its own imbalanced engines. It would orbit this system's sun for years. The fuel cells would take decades to expend. It wasn't a permanent sentence—just an exceptionally long one. When Krev and Azomurn came to their senses, they could await the journey's end in hibernation.

Vythor saw the robot, a red indistinct shape in the sub-warp energies, still clinging to the hull of the vessel.

The escape pod tumbled out of the warp. With a pang of guilt and sadness, Vythor watched the spaceship fade away, disappearing into the sub-dimensional trap as he emerged into real space.

A beautiful planet of blue and green filled the view through the tiny window. Earth. The third planet from the system's star— now safe from the prying scouts of the Haephotian Empire.

The planet's gravity pulled on the pod. Maneuvering rockets fired. The pod adjusted for the angle of re-entry.

Vythor, the alien, descended toward his self-imposed exile.

2. TRAIN WRECK (SEVEN YEARS LATER...)

The Robot stood at the central console. Based on humanoid mobility and function, the Robot was equipped with head, torso, two long arms, and two thin legs. Red highlights rimmed the black composite material of its body. With elongated mechanical fingers, the Robot manipulated a strange keyboard and other input devices.

Various computer banks—some refurbished relics of the past, some extremely advanced—jutted out at intervals along the walls. Wires ran through a central hub, and there were secure wireless transceivers spaced around the room. Perched over the console, a large monitor flashed data and imagery faster than a human eye could take in. Its head tilted upward slightly; the Robot's single rectangular red eye scanned the monitor without interruption.

Sparsely furnished, the lofty abode functioned more as a nerve center than living quarters. Outside, viewed through the panoramic penthouse window, the shining city of Pallas stretched to the shores of Mighty Lake to the east. The north side of the city sprawled out toward suburbs and gently rolling farmlands. Pallas was a city marching toward the future. Clean, bright, futuristic facades mixed with refurbished classic buildings. Dilapidated and downtrodden neighborhoods were rapidly becoming things of the past. City government, civic organizations, philanthropic benefactors—all contributed toward a brighter tomorrow. The Alien's arrival and adoption of Pallas as his home had refocused the city on the potential of the future.

At the Robot's side, in a high-backed chair, the Alien pondered over tented, green fingers. While the Robot was a machine, the Alien was biological and close to being human, except for his green skin and iridescent eyes. The Alien was tall, but not a giant. His frame was etched with powerful muscles. Both the Robot's chest and the Alien's blue shirt displayed the same emblem; a stylized letter from an alien alphabet. Between them, a chess table held a game in progress.

"Not much in the way of crime this morning," the Alien said. He sat still, though his eyes darted, betraying restlessness. "Or any situation where I could be of assistance."

In addition to disrupting criminal activity as a deputized citizen of the city, the Alien also aided victims of catastrophes or disasters around the world when he could. The latter was often difficult because of international bylaws. Still, he had been known to violate a few international treaties—all for the greater good.

No one had yet been able to stop the Alien from helping. Some criminals had tried. Some government agencies had tried, too. Fortunately, the Alien had proven his altruism, and his promises of a peaceful coexistence with humans had borne out.

Of course, there were dissenters. There always were. Those who insisted the Alien was the spearhead of an extraterrestrial invasion. Those who demanded he fully disclose details of his existence before coming to Earth. And there always those on the fringe proffering conspiracy theories: those who thought he was a hoax—a government experiment and now its shadow operative.

The Alien moved the black rook across two spaces. "Check."

The Robot took less than a millisecond to choose its move. Black mechanical fingers slid the remaining white bishop across the board to protect its king. The position of the bishop put the Alien's king in jeopardy.

"Check," the Robot said.

The Alien pondered. "Soon we'll be at stalemate."

"Yes, another impasse. Logical, as you are the one who created me."

"Just because I created you doesn't mean I also dictate your thought processes." The Alien moved his remaining rook again. "Check. Do not forget to think for yourself."

"We are both logical." The Robot moved its king, exposing the Alien's king to a line of attack from his bishop. "This is a game of logic. It is inevitable. Check."

"You're too logical." The Alien retreated the black king, again. "I should take you out in the field with me."

"Why?"

The Alien pursed his lips in thought.

"Human nature is rife with illogic—particularly the criminal element. It needs to be experienced and learned firsthand."

"You are not human," the Robot said. It did not immediately commit another move on the chessboard. "Have you already determined how they behave?"

"Call it humanoid nature, then," the Alien said. "I've had seven years to study and analyze them. They are not too different from my own race."

The Robot was tempted to inquire about the Alien's race. The Robot's data collection algorithm would have been considered a personality trait in a biological, sentient being. Perhaps a trait bordering on obsession. But the Robot had learned not to ask questions about the Alien's past. He never bothered to answer. Sometimes in quieter moments, he would make a statement about his past. Those rare bytes of data were kept on file in the Robot's electronic brain.

"I am a data processor," the Robot said. "Another piece of your equipment in this lair."

"You can be much more." The Alien shook his head. "In the field, your learning could be applied. Your powers of analysis and deduction would benefit."

The Robot's head turned from side to side—a deliberate motion it still practiced. "It would be better for me to remain here. You are better served with me as your nerve center."

The Alien fell into silence and the Robot did not continue the conversation. The chess match continued. As predicted, the next few moves ended the game in stalemate.

After the chess match, the Alien brooded awhile before selecting a volume of poetry from a small stack of books he kept beside his chair. He read silently, though his lips played as if sounding out the rhymes.

The Robot continued its vigil, monitoring the streaming data from Pallas and places beyond. The Alien had talented powers of observation, but even he could not catch and sift every piece of electronic data pouring through the various monitors. The city of the future pulsed with live data. Some feeds were not meant for public consumption. The Robot's hacking skills were formidable, and they were a step above the Alien's talents.

The Robot discovered a distress signal buried among the bytes of data in one of countless streams pouring through the monitoring equipment. Within seconds, the various application windows on the system focused on one situation. Footage from a news helicopter showed a train speeding along its track. Other helicopters would soon follow. Various newsfeeds displayed reporters speaking as captions crawled along the news tickers.

"There is a train out of control," the Robot said.

"Where?" The Alien leaped from his chair, tossed his book into the seat. There was concern on his face and an eagerness in his posture, taut for action. An opportunity to stop idling and act was welcome.

"Southeast-bound track. Pallas-Crowsport line." A map appeared on the monitor. "Acceleration is locked. The driver almost lost control of the train on one curve already."

In the corner of the monitor a black and white video feed appeared. The Robot had hacked into a security camera mounted atop the runaway locomotive. The landscape blurred past, and the railroad tracks pointed away to the horizon.

"Is there enough time?" The Alien would help the victims if the train wrecked, but it would be better to stop the train from crashing at all.

The Robot nodded. "Just enough. You can intercept as the train reaches the suburbs of Crowsport."

A pane of the panoramic window slid open. A forcefield of energy kept the outside weather from entering the penthouse. The energy field was attuned to the Alien's molecular structure and vibrations. The Alien rose into the air and flew across the room, then through the field out the window, eighty-seven stories above the streets of Pallas.

Sweat beaded atop Milton Medina's tanned shaved head, and rivulets ran down his forehead. He took one hand off the handlebar. He grabbed at the end of the towel around his broad shoulders and wiped the moisture before it ran into his eyes. A sweatband would have been more practical, but he thought he looked ridiculous wearing one. His legs pumped the pedals.

The large screen in front of the stationary bicycle gave a visual illusion of riding the Tour De France. In the virtual reality of being halfway up a steep hill, the exercise bike increased resistance. The muscular man strained to maintain his speed. Pushed harder. Milton Medina always pushed harder to reach the top of anything. Anything worth doing, anything worth conquering, took effort.

A frame appeared in the lower corner of the display. A woman with short-cropped red hair appeared in the video feed. She had brown eyes, and she wore a navy blue overshirt with a banded collar.

The man sighed. Luckily for her, he was in a tolerable mood.

"Ms. Kinney. You know I dislike interruptions when I am exercising."

"I'm sorry, sir, I didn't think this news could wait."

"Well?"

"You'll understand."

Another picture-in-picture appeared in the opposite lower corner: a television news broadcast, with the word 'live' displayed under aerial footage of a train speeding along tracks.

The man pulled the speaker buds from his ears, cutting off the audio book he had been listening to.

"...runaway train. Out of control..."

Those were the only phrases he heard. The rest was noise. He knew the train. He knew why his assistant had not said anything more over a communications channel—why she had formally used "sir." He had hired her for her quality of discretion along with a host of other talents he required.

Medina's legs eased up, coming out of the frenzied pedaling, slowing to a calm stop. He stared at the images, listened to another few seconds of the blathering idiots on the news broadcast.

"Thank you, Ms. Kinney."

The woman gave a curt nod. Both the video feeds closed. The vista of the French countryside was whole again, but the landscape stopped passing by when the wheels of the exercise cycle halted.

Without time for a shower, Medina wiped down his body as he strode to his luxurious closet. He forewent formal attire. He donned a basic white tee shirt, black sweatpants, and black sneakers.

He emerged into the mansion's hallway, where his red-headed assistant handed him an electronic tablet bristling with headlines concerning the runaway train.

"This is going to cost me money, Josephine," Medina said.

"Better than going to prison."

"Your concern touches me."

"My concern is tied to your concerns." Josephine grinned. "I could play the innocent, unknowing employee. But then I would be unemployed if anything happened to you."

"There is still a chance nothing incriminating need happen." Medina's finger scrolled through the pad's surface display.

Josephine shook her head.

"I don't see how it won't crash. They can't get control over the computerized accelerator."

Medina pointed to a long shot from a helicopter. A green streak flashed across the sky, almost too fast to be caught on camera.

"The Alien," Josephine said.

"For once, maybe he'll be a help to me rather than a hindrance."

The Alien zoomed across the sky, impervious to the chill wind and high altitude. As an Earth dweller, his extraterrestrial nature had odd side effects. Flight, imperviousness, and amazing strength. Enhanced hearing and vision, as well. He'd had to learn to screen his sensitive hearing, which picked up hundreds of voices. His vision was easier to control, but for a while he'd dealt with vertigo and nausea as his vision had shifted across spectrums. When he'd first arrived on the planet, he had been paradoxically stronger than any human, yet also as helpless as a human baby before he learned to control his powers.

He would have sacrificed all those superpowers to be amongst his own people, on his own world, living a normal life. Well, perhaps not normal. After opportunity to champion and protect people, he wasn't sure he was cut out for a quieter existence. Even though returning to his home planet would mean the loss of his exceptional powers, he was fine with that.

The Alien shook off his ruminations. A train was about to crash, and people were in danger. He needed to focus. One reason he had undertaken the mantle of rescuer had been to shake off thoughts of home. He needed to focus on what he could do on this world of his reluctant exile.

"What kind of train am I dealing with?"

The small device in the Alien's ear was years ahead of current human technology. Along with the audio interface, a micro-camera protruded out to the side to provide video. The Alien had put the device through its paces in the preceding seven years.

"Cargo," the Robot said.

The Alien felt some relief. He only needed to save the crew, not a train full of passengers. Cargo could be replaced. He would try to save the train too, of course, but it would not be the priority. If goods were lost, the owners would need to deal with that. Lives were the priority.

"What kind of cargo?"

"Crude oil."

The Alien grunted. A load full of volatile liquid. Halting the train would be heavy and dangerous work. If any of the tankers ripped open, the potential for fire and pollution would cause further complications.

With heightened eyesight, the Alien spotted the train far ahead. Three maroon and yellow locomotives hauled tanker cars, each one loaded with one hundred thousand liters of flammable fuel. The powerful locomotives sped along. A gradual incline of the terrain did not slow the train's progress.

"I see it," said the Alien. "Do you have its position in real time?"

Data feeds could be slow, but the Robot had an arsenal of tricks and equipment to work around such issues.

"Nearly." The Robot paused to confirm. "Yes. The current track incline stops in two hundred yards. The track then declines. There is another curve near the bottom. You must reach the train before it gets there."

"Area surrounding the curve?"

"Residential neighborhood," the Robot replied.

The Alien gazed farther down the track, his vision penetrating with x-rays and other spectrums unknown to the human eye. People and automobiles were in the streets. Police were attempting to force order on the chaos.

"It hasn't been evacuated."

"No, they are trying but the train is coming much too fast. The evacuation will still be in progress."

The Alien flattened his arms against the sides of his body. He angled downward and fell into a rapid descent. The wind whistled in his ears. As he neared the top of the train, he curved his trajectory upward until he paralleled the ground. He shot along the length of the train toward the locomotives.

His options were limited. He had no more time for consulting the Robot. Following his first instinct, the Alien sped ahead of the train, turned, and faced the oncoming engine. Through the besmirched windows, the Alien saw three engineers. One frantically worked the controls. The other two argued. Their faces showed fear and anger. The lead engineer looked up and spotted the Alien. He hollered and pointed a finger. Forgetting their argument for the moment, the other men looked out the windscreen.

Facing backward, the Alien appeared standing in air, but he kept his body moving, matching the train's speed. He didn't truly fly; he had the ability to defy gravity. He could hover stationary anywhere in the air.

He reached out his hands and placed them against the front of the locomotive. A jarring impact would be as disastrous as taking the curve too fast. Slowly, he increased his resistance against the speeding train. Muscles taut, rippling under his green skin, the Alien pushed against the engine. He grimaced with effort as he felt the speed and weight exerting pressure through his body.

The train needed more drag to slow down. He shifted downward, let his feet reach the ground, and braced one leg out behind his body. Dirt clouded into the air, rocks flew, and wooden railroad ties splintered with mighty cracks of giants' bones breaking as the Alien plowed a tremendous furrow through the earth.

As the cross ties shattered, the integrity of the train track gave way. The gap between the rails widened, and the train's wheels met raw, torn ground. The friction of impact helped to slow the train. The Alien redoubled his effort. The spinning wheels of the locomotives chewed earth and wood, also contributing to the train's deceleration.

The train slowed down, but not quickly enough.

The Alien felt the locomotive lifting on one side, threatening to roll over. He pressed his shoulder against the train and leaned his body into the effort. With lighting speed and implausible strength, his free hand punched a hole in the side of the locomotive. Using the hole for a handgrip, he attempted to hold the train upright. Metal screeched and tore; his hand came away with a piece.

The three locomotives jackknifed. The Alien glanced over his shoulder. He saw suburban rooftops and residential streets. People in those streets were abandoning cars stuck in the chaotic traffic jam and running for their lives away from the railroad tracks. Panicked, they ran in all directions.

The Alien mustered his strength and pressed against the train. He pushed at an angle, roughly pulling the cinching train off its trajectory. He shoved, pushed upward, and the first locomotive lifted its nose into the air. His grip crushed handholds within the folded, bent metal. He lifted into the air, pulling the train upward until all three locomotives were off the ground. The tanker cars tilted and twisted. Some car couplings snapped.

Everything smashed in a tearing, rolling crash. Small trees splintered under heavy impact. The locomotives flipped onto their sides, wheels still spinning furiously. Some of the tankers lost their structural integrity and ripped open. Crude oozed out of their torn sides, blackening the ground.

"That blundering fool!" Medina slammed his fist on the desk. On the television screen in the corner of his office, the live newscast had shown the Alien stopping the train, lifting the twisted debris of the locomotive into the air. Wrecked tankers gushed oil.

"He has stopped it from crashing," Josephine said.

"A crash would have more easily covered my trail." Medina stared at the single button remote control on his desk. He reached for it, pulled his hand back. He drummed his fingers on the table. He had prepared for the worst-case scenario, but he was hesitant to engage his precautions. How could he not have foreseen the Alien's involvement? This now might be the worst case, and he had overlooked the possibility of the scenario he faced. He felt foolish. It was not a familiar feeling. It was uncomfortable.

"What else can you do?" Josephine asked.

Medina gritted his teeth. "But if he's there...."

"Either way, Milton," Josephine said. They were in private and speaking directly to each other. Medina allowed the familiarity. "You can't let there be evidence."

"This will bring the Alien down on me, Josephine. Mark my words." Medina said.

"You've always covered your tracks, Milton. Quite well."

He wasn't sure if she was speaking with honesty or flattery. It sounded like both. She was smart enough to know flattery was useless.

"I've been studying the Alien ever since he arrived." Medina shook his head. His instincts told him he would leave a trail this time. "I've been working around him the best I can. I knew we'd come up against each other eventually, but I have the feeling the day has now come."

The Alien surveyed the residential neighborhood. No wreckage had reached the houses, but oil flowed toward them. Fire trucks, red lights flashing and sirens blaring, were approaching. The Alien looked inside the lead locomotive. The crewmembers were dazed. They had been tossed around. Two were bleeding, one was not moving. The safety glass was easier to punch through than the metal had been. The Alien tore out the glass panes and climbed inside.

He reached for a staggering engineer, who was wiping a torrent of blood out of his eyes. The man had a deep gash on his forehead.

"I'm all right. Just a bad cut." The man waved him away. "Check on the others."

The other conscious engineer bled from a compound fracture of him upper arm. Though the Alien scooped him up as gently as he could, the man let out a cry and fainted. The Alien flew out of the locomotive. He searched the scene until he saw a cluster of ambulances.

The Alien descended. One paramedic—possibly new to the city and unfamiliar with the Alien—stood slack-jawed. The Alien didn't know the other paramedic, but she must have been a veteran of medical service in Pallas. His arrival from the sky carrying a wounded man didn't faze her in the least.

The Alien placed the engineer on a waiting gurney.

"Are there others?" asked the woman. She was tall and muscular with blonde hair.

"Two. One is unconscious," the Alien said. "One had a cut and claims to be well, but I will bring him, too."

"Better let me check the unconscious one before you move him."

The Alien gave her a smile.

"What is your name?"

"Kate."

"Very well, Kate." The Alien grabbed the paramedic and took to the air.

She let out a whoop.

"Problem with heights?"

"No!" She grinned. "Just not the ambulance ride I expected this evening."

Arriving at the locomotive, Kate squeezed her eyes shut as the Alien flew in through the opening where the windshield had been. Once inside, the paramedic went to work. She handed a pad of sterile gauze to the engineer with the forehead injury. "Keep pressure on it."

Kate knelt to examine his unconscious colleague. She probed with fingers along his extremities. The man groaned. "Well, let's hope that's a good sign. Nothing broken." Kate looked around the cabin, noted the mess. "Probably plenty of bruises and abrasions, though."

The Alien breathed out in relief and exhaustion. The crew would be all right. The neighborhood populace and buildings were not smashed. The train was wrecked, though. Who knew what environmental impact the oil would have? He hoped cleanup crews were among the civic professionals arriving. At least nothing had sparked a fire.

Medina toyed with the remote as the drama played out on the screen. He wasn't sure why he was waiting. There would be no ideal moment. Maybe, if he had been at the crash site personally, he could make a better judgement, but he didn't have the luxury. He had the disparate public news sources and nothing more.

He should have had some of his own people on the train. He would not make that mistake again. Again? He would need to setup an entirely new operation after this debacle.

"Josephine," Medina said, calm returning to his voice. "Schedule a luncheon appointment for me with Mr. Dufresne in Crowsport, won't you?"

Josephine was already accessing the calendar on her phone. "What shall I say is the reason for your visit?"

"We have some details to iron out in our working relationship." Medina rubbed his thumb along the top of the remote. "We need to discuss financial reparations."

Medina pressed the button.

The Alien grimaced as a high-pitched whine sliced through the other noises of the disaster. The ground shook. A blast of sound and orange light erupted somewhere down the ruined track. The Alien exited the locomotive and looked along the train tracks. One of the tanker cars had exploded, flames billowing outward. The flames spread quickly along the ground and black smoke columned into the sky. With all the spilled oil, there would be an inferno if the blaze hopped from car to car.

"Registering a seismic disturbance." The Robot's voice was in the Alien's ear again. "Did one of the tanker cars explode?"

"Yes, but there weren't any flames or sparks to...."

Farther down, a second tanker exploded. Another column of flame, burning splotches of fuel shot through the air, threatening to ignite numerous smaller blazes.

"Another," the Robot reported.

The Alien flew over wreckage of the train.

"That car was derailed but not compromised." The Alien observed.

"Analyzing," the Robot said.

The Alien shook his head.

"Are you hearing that sound? A high-pitched whine."

"Negative," said the Robot.

The Alien pressed a finger against the device in his ear.

"Anything wrong with the comm system?"

"Negative."

Another explosion erupted close enough to buffet the Alien. His body and unique clothing were impervious to the flames, but the shockwave sent him cartwheeling through the air. He shielded his eyes with his forearm to block shrapnel. He couldn't see, but the micro camera in his earpiece relayed a fisheye view back to the Robot.

"Pattern established," the Robot said. "Analysis of your video indicates the explosion emanated from the interior of the cars."

"Explosives in the oil tankers," the Alien said. "The whine I'm hearing..."

"...is a signal," the Robot agreed.

"Coming from a remote detonator!"

"That is the most likely conclusion."

The Alien increased his speed. Another tanker car exploded, somewhere ahead. Not every car seemed targeted. The explosions would finish before he could locate the source of the signal. He would need to make a fortunate grab.

"Is there a pattern to the explosions?"

To the naked eye, the Alien was a blur. At his own pace, the world around slowed. A few of the destroyed cars had exploded simultaneously, but most were exploding in sequence along the train. The Alien had a slight chance to reach the final targeted tanker with enough time to perform his task.

The Robot found the pattern.

"Every third tanker."

The Alien reached the tanker car which would be the last to explode—if the Robot had calculated correctly. With blurring speed, he spun open its fluid release valves. The crude oil wasn't evacuating quickly enough.

He leaped to the top of the tanker and spun the hatch wheel to open the dome access lid. He took a deep breath, closed his eyes, and dove into the inky darkness.

As he groped through the thick, caustic crude, his vision spectrum shifted through his eyelids. He saw a vague outline of an object lying at the bottom of the car. He reached for the object and felt something solid in the goopy liquid. He grabbed hold, flew up and out of the tanker car.

Hovering above the tanker car, wiping the crude from his eyes, the Alien gazed down at his prize. A hermetically sealed bag concealed a rectangular container about one meter long. He tore away the bag, revealing a wooden crate.

He punched a hole in the top of the crate. The hole showed an intriguing sight, but the Alien only had a glimpse; a microsecond to commit the image to memory. A metal fin. A tubed body.

An unmarked missile.

A blinking red light on the warhead.

He dropped the crate, turned away, but could not escape before the missile exploded. Even the Alien could not ignore the effect of the shockwave. Momentarily dazed, he realized he had been blasted through the air. His body felt heat from the blazing tanker car as his mind struggled through disorientation. Hot shards of the missile he had held ignited the fuel through the opening at the top of the tanker car.

The Alien hit the ground hard. After a moment, he recovered his senses and propped himself up on his elbow. Smoke roiled over the scene. More fire trucks and police cars were arriving, sirens wailing and colored lights flashing. Somewhere overhead, helicopter rotors whirred.

Static sounded in his ear.

"All... ri..."

The disruption surprised the Alien. His earpiece was designed and manufactured to withstand abuse. The explosion had been powerful. Taking a swim in the oil might have affected the device, too.

"I am all right," The Alien reported. "I don't know if you can hear me, but my earpiece is compromised."

"Shif... freq..."

"Never mind." The Alien shook his head.

"Shifting frequencies" The Robot's transmission was clear again.

"Good work," the Alien said. "I wonder how much more this communicator can take. I'll need to build a new one soon."

"Video analysis was lost when you dove into the tanker car," the Robot said. "It is still offline."

"There was a crate. In the crate was a missile." The Alien wiped his arm. His grimy hand smeared more oil than it removed. The excess sluiced off. He would need a good shower. "Compact design. Small and powerful. Designed for surface-to-air, I would guess."

"Illegal armaments."

"Yes. Smuggling." The Alien stood up and groaned. He stared at the flames and carnage for a few moments.

"It appears you have a crime to investigate after all," the Robot said.

Despite his discomfort, the Alien grinned.

"Yes. Yes, I do."

3. A MYSTERIOUS CALL

The Robot turned the device over in its fingers. On the workbench, tools and micro-electronic pieces were laid out in an orderly fashion. The device was stained, scratched, and scorched. The Robot pried open the casing; loose bits fell out onto the bench top.

"I am not sure repairs can be affected on this audio-video unit," the Robot said.

The video circuits had been completed destroyed. Though the frequency shift had given them a clear conversation, it was short lived. The audio had failed while the Alien had spent the rest of the afternoon assisting with recovery efforts.

"I figured I would need to make a new one," the Alien said. "But I'm not sure I have enough materials left."

"You could make the device from human technology."

"True, but it wouldn't be as durable or reliable." The Alien crossed his arms and took a long gaze at the Robot.

"I think you will be my direct eyes and ears for the time being," the Alien said. "It's time for you to do field work."

The Robot angled his head slightly, a movement it did when pondering. "If you believe it to be necessary."

"The recordings of my exploits are not vanity," the Alien said. "I am a stranger in a strange world. Analysis helps me to better my interactions with humanity. It also shows the authorities the justification for my actions. It helps to strengthen their trust in me."

The newsfeeds flashing through the data center of the Alien's lair focused on the train crash. Details, news reports, hacked government reports—local and federal. Interviews with eyewitnesses. The main crew conductor had given one interview, and then under legal advisement, kept away from the media.

The Alien stood up from his chair and paced.

"The Pallas-Crowsport line and many other rail companies in the circle of influence of Crowsport lead to the unnamed crime syndicate operated by mob boss Charles Dufresne," the Robot said.

"I know about the trains and Dufresne. Crowsport is not my jurisdiction. I'll get to him in time. I'm more interested in the manufacturer of those missiles."

The Robot turned its square eye, briefly forgoing its data intake to observe the flashing screen in front of the Alien. The Alien scanned through records concerning Dufresne. Faces, reports, newspaper articles, online stories. Some data was public, some was not. Some information came to the penthouse lair through arrangements with law enforcement, while the clandestine feeds came without official sanction.

A strange face flicked by. The Robot analyzed and replayed the face it its own memory.

"Please go back."

The Alien obliged.

"There."

The photograph on the screen showed a human female with a snouted black nose and copious fur growing on her face. Her mouth curled in a permanent feral snarl.

"Dog Woman," the Alien said. He nonchalantly continued scanning criminal profiles.

"Dog. Woman," the Robot said. The terms did not belong together. "I did not know lycanthropy was a real affliction."

"It's not," the Alien said. "She was—is—Doctor Janice Stendahl. A genius in genetics. Experimented on herself."

"At least she kept her experiments confined to herself."

The Alien shook his head. "Initially. She branched out soon enough. When I stopped her, she was attempting to create a pack of creatures like herself. She had an overwhelming need for companionship—and the need to be the alpha wolf."

"This incident is not in the main records."

"Some of my earlier adventures were off the record." The Alien grinned. "Very off the record."

"If I haven't found it in my data perusals, then I would agree," the Robot said. "Very off the record."

The Alien continued scanning through mugshots, portraits, and candid photographs of Dufresne's criminal gang and associates. He expanded the search beyond Crowsport, finding other mobsters of Dufresne's level and influence. A few leads appeared in Pallas. In the past, there had been more. Organized crime was on the run in the Shining City, partly due to the Alien's crimefighting efforts.

"Any analysis on the explosive residue?"

The Robot looked at the monitors. "No. If it has been analyzed, the report has not reached any system we are monitoring."

"It was a long shot. The explosions and burning fuel expunged any clues. The perfect cover if something went wrong."

"We must wait for more evidence."

"Not necessarily. We can take a leap of logic," the Alien said. "Dufresne came up through the crime syndicate the old-fashioned way. He is an old-fashioned thinker."

"Meaning?"

"Dufresne is not technical." The Alien's fingers ran over the keyboard. "I saw a portion of the missile. I heard the self-destruct signal. It's not simple weaponry. We need to find a technical thread."

"There." The Alien pointed to the screen. A man with a buzz haircut smiled awkwardly at the camera, thick-rimmed eyeglasses too big for his face. The knot of his tie skewed to one side, and the pocket of his striped short-sleeve shirt contained a pocket protector loaded with pens and pencils.

The Robot read the name. "Alan Stumper."

"He was an accountant for Dufresne. Handy with numbers and computers."

"Where is he now?"

"Dead—to the rest of the world, anyway. If I recall correctly, there were strange circumstances. He had been embezzling from Dufresne."

"So, Dufresne had him murdered?"

"Dufresne thinks he did. Died two years ago." The Alien snapped his fingers. He typed rapidly. "Cross-referencing against all tech-firm hiring in the Pallas vicinity in the past two years."

The data on the screen superimposed the known photograph of Stumper over another face. A robust beard, long stringy hair, and low-profile wire-rimmed eyeglasses had altered his outward appearance to a large degree.

The Robot read the name under the composite image. "Nate Fulcrum."

"It's Stumper. I'm sure it is."

"He works for M. M. Labs," the Robot reported. "Milton Medina's company?"

"Medina's research division, yes. He secretly owns or controls many businesses." The Alien furrowed his eyebrows. "Which is one reason I've kept an eye on him. I don't trust a man who works in secret."

"You and I have some secrets," the Robot said.

"We're not men."

The Robot recognized the ironic humor in the Alien's statement. The recognition surprised the Robot. The concept of humor was difficult, but the Robot was learning. Perhaps the Robot could work outside the Lair, among humans.

"Did the government put Stumper in witness protection?"

"Yes. Medina was willing and able to provide the man with a job." The Alien rubbed his chin. "Medina is a tech wizard. Almost a match for us. He would have had access to the same data at the time."

"How were you able to get M. M. Labs' employment data? Medina's networks are far too secure. I have never been able to penetrate even his first levels of firewall and protection."

"Because this isn't from Medina's systems," the Alien said. "It's from an online job search site. The entry is two years old and offline. Stumper—Fulcrum—must have put it out there before Medina hired him."

The Robot studied the face on the screen. "You would think a man in hiding would be more careful."

"Ego is a human problem. He probably didn't believe Dufresne would have any reason to search online job sites. Mobsters don't generally hire through the web."

"How is Stumper the link? He would not have introduced the two men," the Robot said. "Dufresne would kill him."

"Stumper isn't the link; he is a weapon. He knows too much about Dufresne." The Alien shrugged. "My guess would be Medina used Stumper's knowledge to force Dufresne to cooperate."

"Would Medina—as they say—play his hand so blatantly? What would keep Dufresne from attempting to kill Stumper again?"

"Medina doesn't need to say a word about Stumper. He can use Stumper's information to leverage Dufresne. And he can keep Stumper in check by threatening to tip Dufresne."

"If your suspicions are true, it appears Medina is a man with patience," the Robot said. "He protected Stumper for two years to have this upper hand now."

"I suspect Medina's been up to no good for a while, and we're just discovering the fact."

The screen displayed the image of a handsome man, swarthy and bald. The photograph was an outtake from a magazine cover shoot. He was well dressed, and his expression was serious with a hint of a smile at the corner his mouth.

"Milton Medina."

"That is hard to believe," the Robot said. "On the surface, Medina is interested in moving the city into the future as you are. He is all about public relations and altruism."

"He has the resources to put together those missiles and ship them illegally."

"There are many factories and technologically advanced companies in Pallas."

"Most with direct or indirect ties to him," the Alien said. "Many of them have the resources to produce the weapons, but only Medina has the money and resources to keep it all quiet and under the radar."

"Why would he? He needs no money from illegal dealings."

"I don't know why," the Alien said. "You find human nature

confusing. I assure you it is. I have been at it a while, and I am often perplexed."

"Are you going to interview Stumper?"

"Eventually," the Alien said. He studied Medina's smiling image. "I might start with Medina himself, though I'm certain he will reveal nothing. We're going to need to tread carefully if we want to prove Milton Medina—shining citizen and Pallas's most successful businessman—is a criminal mastermind."

Crowsport was everything the city of Pallas was not. Pallas was the future; Crowsport was trapped in a sprawl of urban decay and gothic skyscrapers. Pallas felt bright under sunshine. Crowsport reveled in shadows. Even during the day certain streets swallowed pedestrians in dark alleys.

On one such darkened daytime street, Milton Medina stepped from his limousine. He wore a trim, flattering white suit, black belt, and black shoes. His lime green shirt and a purple bow tie added a splash of color to his ensemble. Josephine, serving as Medina's limousine driver, closed the door.

They surveyed the rusted, faded sign over the darkened windows of the restaurant: JACQUES'S BISTRO.

"It looks like a dump," Josephine said. "Do you want some antacids?"

"I hear it has the best French food in the city," Medina said. "Looks can be deceiving."

"I'll stay with the limo." Josephine took off her cap and ruffled her red hair, then perched the cap back on her head, brim askew.

The dilapidated facade of the eatery belied its interior. Though dimly lit, Medina saw the dark woodwork shined with polish and attention. The cooking food smelled enticing. A young blonde hostess led Medina to a table.

The only customer in the entire restaurant was a heavy-set man with a thin mustache. A napkin stuffed in his shirt collar, the man's noticeable paunch met the edge of the table where he sat. The dearth of customers could not be attributed to the hour, nor the quality of food, nor the lack of service. The restaurant had been ordered to remain empty, and so it had.

Before the large suit-clad man could rise to offer a greeting, Medina impetuously sat in the chair across from him. He snatched up the menu and scanned the selections.

"You don't need to be rude," said Dufresne.

The busboy poured water into Medina's glass.

Medina took a long sip of water before responding. "At this point in our relationship, Dufresne, I believe formalities can be dropped."

"You're late."

"Maybe if you'd backed off skimming the city toll booths, I would have arrived on time."

Dufresne glanced nervously at the retreating back of the busboy.

"Careful when you talk about my business."

Medina smiled. He should have laughed. As a mobster, Dufresne worked with intimidation. Nothing had ever intimidated Milton Medina.

"Please. You made sure the place was empty. The staff know enough not to hear a single word we say."

"Why did you call this meeting, Medina?"

"Your train crashed."

"You blew it up!"

"I disposed of incriminating evidence—as a necessity to protect both of our organizations."

"You owe me," Dufresne said. He pointed a pudgy finger across the table.

"I owe you? I hired you," Medina said. "I hired you to ensure my cargo was safely transported to Crowsport for shipping. Your engineer got excited, jumpy. He should never have been going so fast. You're lucky I'm not demanding a refund."

"Who are you to demand anything of me?"

"Your client, for one thing."

"I don't like being talked to the way you're talking to me."

Medina laughed. "Take your big bad mob-boss act somewhere else, Dufresne. You don't intimidate me."

"Maybe you won't get out that door alive."

"If I don't show up in Pallas in the next few days for my board meetings," Medina pointed his finger down and pressed it to the table, "my trail will lead authorities right here."

Dufresne took a dinner roll from the basket, glanced around the restaurant. "Here? Nothing here. Who would tell?"

"My assistant."

"The pretty one, in the car?" Dufresne's smile was as hollow as a jack o' lantern.

There was a knock on the door. Through the blurry glass, Medina saw shadows. If he squinted, the shape could have been a lolling head of a body hanging over an arm.

Dufresne waved to an underling. "I think there is a package at the door. Robert was going to retrieve it from Mr. Medina's car. Open the door."

The lackey pulled open the front door.

A limp body slammed against him. The lackey and the body tumbled to the floor. The limp body—presumably, Robert—bled profusely. The doorway framed Josephine's lithe form, bloodied Bowie knife in hand. She flashed a wicked grin.

Dufresne leapt up, screaming, shouting, swearing, and pointing. Before anyone acted, Medina pounced with lightning speed. A few well-placed punches and open hand chops left Dufresne on the floor, clutching his throat, gasping for air.

"You think I'm some soft businessman in a suit?" Medina said. "I could crack you open like an egg, Dufresne! I could send your whole organization down in flames if it wasn't convenient for me to keep your infrastructure running for my own ends. I should let Josephine slit you like a hog!"

Busboys and waiters grabbed for pistols concealed in their smocks. A man in a dirty white apron balled his fists.

"Next one who moves dies," Josephine said. Her bloody knife had been replaced with a machine pistol.

Dufresne held up a hand, waved his people to stand down.

"All right," Dufresne gasped. "All right. Everyone back to your business."

The mobster heaved his shaking body onto his chair.

"Just a disagreement," the mob boss insisted. His crew stood down and retreated into the kitchen and other stations.

"A disagreement." Medina smiled cordially. "Let's order dinner and discuss business. May Josephine join us? She's here anyway now. I'm sure my limousine will be left unmolested so long as I am in your establishment."

"No problem," Dufresne said. "On both counts."

Most of the dinner conversation consisted of small talk, long gaps of silence, and ignoring the removal and cleanup of the stabbed gangster. The nervous staff brought various courses, whispering harshly at each other whenever Dufresne, Medina, or Josephine gave the slightest look of disapproval. They did their jobs well, though. Some seemed far more comfortable carrying trays than guns.

Medina forked wine-poached salmon into his mouth. The black truffles were a delight. "Pity this restaurant is your private establishment, Dufresne. It would do all right as its own business."

"I've thought about it." Dufresne scowled. "Tough neighborhood, though."

"Crime is a problem everywhere." Medina nodded and changed the subject.

"The Alien saved the train. Did he see anything?"

"He saw the explosions," Dufresne said. "Up close and personal, I hear. Unfortunately, it didn't kill him."

"Did he see anything incriminating?"

"I don't know."

"You have contacts on the police force; find out what they know."

Dufresne swirled his wine in the glass. "They've been clamming up lately."

"Why?"

"Some vigilante type. Calls himself 'The Protector.' Ha. He's running in criminals and crooked cops. Thinks he's like that Alien of yours." Dufresne curled his lip in a mean grin. "No upstart is gonna run me off my own turf."

"I know how you feel now that the Alien finally stuck his nose in my business."

"That's been comin' awhile," the mobster said. "I mean, him being all spaceman futuristic and all. Really cut in on your master of future technology schtick with the city fathers, didn't it?"

Medina ignored the verbal jab. He changed the subject.

"In hindsight, my previous shipment was optimistic. You must have extra missiles. You better empty your warehouse."

"Are you telling me how to do my job?"

"The Alien is a clever one. He'll trace something to you. I don't want the trail going any further."

Dufresne relented, put his hands in the air. "I'll get it moved."

"Not just moved; dispose of it."

"It's not easy. I don't get invited to the bomb range on weekends."

"Suit yourself," Medina said. "But remote detonators are equipped on every missile I make. I have private satellites, so don't think they can be moved out of range. It's a feature. If the ordnance falls into the hands of enemies or terrorists...." Medina's thumb curled down on his fist.

"Boom?"

"Boom." Medina smiled. "Its a special frequency and code, set to the buyer's choice. Of course, I can override their code. I can explode them anytime. And with my technology, from almost anywhere."

Medina pulled a black, single-button remote from his pocket.

"Is that...?"

"It is."

"Don't! You'll waste my warehouse and my people." Dufresne waved at the device, signaling Medina to put it away. "I'll get rid of them—but that's a lot of money to throw away."

"Don't even think of trying to sell those missiles on the black market, Dufresne. I wouldn't be happy. You saw what happens when I'm not happy."

"Yes," Dufresne said. "We all saw. Why would you let all those missiles go without a fight?"

"A man needs to pick his battles," Medina said. "This is too incriminating. I love risks. It's not the money, it's the risk—but this is too close. I'm not ready to go to prison. I don't think you are either."

"No, I'm not," said Dufresne. "So, you don't need the money.

You break the law for the thrill of it. You're a thrill seeker."

"I suppose I am. It's deeper than you would understand."

"Of course it is." Dufresne sneered.

"I misspoke." Medina held up a hand. "I have trouble explaining what it means to me in ways other people can understand."

"You're paying me to handle your stuff," Dufresne said. "Not be your therapist. Are we done here?"

Medina swirled the water in his glass, gulped down the last drops, and crunched the last sliver of ice between his teeth.

"We're done here."

Medina watched the autumn scenery roll past as the limousine ate up the straight miles of turnpike between Crowsport and Pallas. Normally, he would be working—making calls, checking in remotely. The train wreck and Dufresne's incompetence were distracting. Medina meditated on other channels he could attempt to exploit. He had sold many illegal armaments. They needed to be smuggled out of the country to reach their destinations and impatient buyers.

He shook his head. He had enough money. Why bother?

The game. To game the game, as he had told Dufresne. To win and laugh at every law he skirted because he could. He was Milton Medina. No one would tell him what he could or could not do.

"You might have had your talk with Dufresne a little too early," Josephine said, intruding on his reverie.

"What makes you say that?"

Josephine ruffled her right hand in the leather satchel on the passenger seat. She handed a computer tablet over her shoulder.

Medina examined the spreadsheet on the display. An inventory report had entries highlighted in red, and notes had been added.

"I noticed the discrepancy while I was waiting in the car before those idiots tried something."

Medina grunted. "You should have told me."

"Sorry. I figured you were already irked about the missiles and the train." Josephine kept her eyes focused on the road ahead. "I thought bringing it up at the table with Dufresne might not be the smartest thing to do."

Medina rubbed his large hand over his shaved head, read the data again.

He was missing a laser. To be more precise, a laser had disappeared from one of Medina's research and development units. A routine inventory check had revealed the theft.

A special laser, too. Not one with a military purpose, but a new design—powerful, to be marketed for industrial use. He would augment the design for military use soon enough.

There was hardly a black market for lasers. This theft stank of industrial sabotage. But who? Medina had removed all tech rivals from Pallas. It had to be someone from somewhere else. Plans were usually easier to steal than a physical machine, but Medina's tech security was perhaps the best in the world.

But he employed as much physical security as technological security. No employee could simply stroll out of work at the end of the day with an industrial laser tucked under their arm. If the thieves worked from outside, they must have had some help from the inside, too.

The idea he'd been betrayed put a cold stone of anger in his guts.

"Josephine, I want you to compile a list of employees." Was it his imagination, or did he notice Josephine sit up a little straighter, as if sensing the icy fury in his belying calm voice? "Sniff out who has money issues, family issues, problems at home, or an attitude at work."

Medina wouldn't employ anyone who was a liability, but circumstances could change. He couldn't keep tabs on every worker all the time. Perhaps they were due for a full audit, worldwide.

"Understood." Josephine gave a curt nod. "Do you want me to take care of it, or do you want to talk with them once I find them?"

Medina glowered out the window, saw red rather than the scenery passing. Who would have the audacity?

"Oh, I will certainly need to talk to them personally."

The Alien had a strong urge to confront Medina. Perhaps he would fly over the billionaire's mansion gates and force the front door. He suspected Medina would shrug at such an entrance. The Alien had no hard evidence; a confrontation would yield nothing. He decided to play straight and direct.

He did not, however, contact the business mogul ahead of time to arrange an appointment.

The Alien swooped down to the gate. The motion cameras followed his movements.

He pressed the call button.

A woman's voice came over the speaker.

"State your name."

"I am the Alien."

The information did not faze the woman.

"Do you have an appointment with Mr. Medina?"

"I don't," confessed the Alien. "But I am hoping he can fit me in. I'd like to discuss the train wreck."

"What does Mr. Medina have to do with the train...."

The Alien heard a muffled voice, perhaps somewhere behind the woman. There was a pause.

"Very well." There was a snippiness to her tone. The Alien did not believe her attitude was directed at him.

The gates slid open. The Alien walked along the drive. He could have flown to the door, but he wanted to survey the grounds. Perhaps his lazy approach would irritate Medina. Irritation might put the man off his game.

The grounds were trimmed and well kept. No tree had overgrown its welcome. Small flower gardens and bush formations dotted the landscape. At the end of the drive, to the left, a large carport stood. The canvas and plastic windowed sides of the structure were rolled up, proudly displaying a collection of automobiles.

At the steps of the mansion, a woman in a Nehru jacket awaited his arrival. She wore her red hair short. Boots and tan riding pants completed her ensemble. She seemed equally ready to serve as a chauffeur as for a day of horseback riding.

"I am Ms. Kinney," she said. She had found her smile,

though the Alien suspected it grated her to do so. "Assistant to Mr. Medina. Please follow me."

The Alien was led through wide, spartan corridors. A glimpse through an open door showed a library, a small gym, a personal theater. The Alien might have used his enhanced visual abilities to see through the closed doors, but he had trained himself to use those powers only when absolutely needed. He might see any number of things, but the law required proper procedure. Evidence seized without warrants was inadmissible in court.

Every citizen had a right to privacy—and a fair trial.

Ms. Kinney escorted him into an office. A large oak desk dominated the center of the room. Behind the desk, Milton Medina rose from his chair. He wore a tailored tan suit and dark brown shirt. He extended a hand.

"Pleasure to meet you at last."

The Alien shook the hand. Medina was strong, no idle desk jockey. There was fierceness in the man's eyes.

"I've seen you at a charity event or two, but we've never had the chance to speak," the Alien said.

Medina nodded. "I often make my appearance and then make my exit soon after. Too much to do."

"The quintessential businessman?" asked the Alien. "Always busy with the corporation."

"The Medina Corporation needs a strong hand. We need to maintain what we have and stretch to meet new challenges."

The Alien curved his mouth in a half smile. "Like missiles."

Medina didn't blink or flinch. The Alien filtered his super-sensitive hearing, but Medina's heart did not skip a beat or change pace.

"Armaments are one of my corporation's many products. But why are we discussing those?"

"The train crash and explosion last week."

"It must have been a terrible crash to ignite all that oil." Medina pointed out a window. "I could see the plume of black smoke from here."

"I mitigated most of the damage," the Alien said. "The tankers exploded because they were smuggling missiles. The missiles exploded."

"And you think they were my missiles? That's why you're here?"

"Yes."

"Well," Medina shrugged. "They were my missiles."

The Alien was surprised. Had Medina just nonchalantly confessed?

"Those missiles were stolen from my warehouse eight days ago," Medina explained.

The Alien couldn't help feeling he was hearing an orchestrated alibi. Medina's candor had him off-guard. He wasn't sure how to proceed.

"Stolen? I hadn't heard."

"Of course, you wouldn't have. Do you want a panic on our hands? Missiles on the loose, potentially reaching the hands of terrorists—right here at home?"

"I'm sure you feel bad," the Alien said.

Medina nodded his head, while his facial expression and body language conveyed a different attitude toward the affair. He leaned over the laptop on his desk, tapped at the keyboard, and spun the screen toward the Alien.

"A laser was stolen, too. An important project to me. Then again, all my projects are important to me."

That was a curious addendum. Any number of people might want missiles, but a laser, too?

The Alien read the emails and scans of various communications with law enforcement, military, and government agencies. They indicated Medina had reported the theft of his armaments in a timely fashion. There was no mention of the missing laser, however.

"They mustn't be happy with you," the Alien said.

"Perhaps not, but I supply products to them all. They can't rake me over the coals too harshly."

"And the laser?"

"Ah." Medina gave a chagrined smile. "We only recently determined that. It's purposed for industry, not military, anyway."

Documents could be forged. The Alien would make his own inquiries. It was curious the Robot hadn't hacked the data, but

Medina was a formidable technologist. If he had wanted the theft kept secret, it would have been kept secret.

"Like you—from what I've heard and read—I prefer digital data." Medina pointed to a printer in the corner. "But if you want print-outs to take with you...."

"That won't be necessary."

"Is there anything else I can do for you?"

"No." The Alien smiled. "Not for now. I'm sure you're busy and I've taken too much of your time."

"My thought exactly, but as your host it would have been rude of me to say so."

Medina escorted the Alien out onto the grounds, near the car park. The Alien admired the mix of antique automobiles and higher-end newer models.

"Thank you for your time, Mr. Medina."

Medina shook his hand, pumped the Alien's arm with a strong grip.

"Please. You are a servant of the city of Pallas, but you don't need to be a humble servant in my presence. Call me Milton."

The Alien nodded.

"Milton," he said. The informality felt awkward. "Until next time."

"Until next time."

The Alien flew up and away into the sky.

When he glanced down, he saw Medina still standing on the front lawn, a studious expression on his face, watching him depart.

Medina turned and pursed his lips. He wasn't sure he should have mentioned the laser. But why not? The Alien was bound to continue to dig around despite Medina's assurances. Josephine's internal audit of employees had not yielded a clue. No security alarms had been tripped. The thief had come and gone with the laser like some ghost. Maybe the Alien would turn something up. Law abiding citizens had their uses, too.

He met Josephine on her way out the front door.

"I need to run errands," she said.

"By all means."

"Or would you rather I stay to talk about...?" She looked upward.

"No, keep to our schedules. Everything is business as usual at the mansion and with Medina Corporation."

Josephine nodded her understanding. She opted for the black van as opposed to the black limousine for her jaunt. She drove off with a wave of her gloved hand.

Medina's shoes clacked along the palatial corridors of his mansion. He settled in his office chair, tented his fingers, and pondered his next move.

A muffled ringtone sounded from the desk drawer. Medina raised his eyebrows. He pulled open the drawer and stared at the cellphone display. The number was secured three times over, including protection from Medina's own communications network. Only Josephine had the number.

The caller ID showed nothing at all.

The phone continued to ring. It should have cut to voicemail after eight rings. Somehow the setting was being overridden.

Medina picked up the phone gingerly, as if it might burn his fingers. He thought about not saying anything, waiting to hear the voice on the other end. But his curiosity was piqued, and he spoke first.

"Medina here."

"I understand you had an unwelcome visitor a few moments ago."

A masking device disguised the voice, giving it a metallic edge.

"Who is this?"

"I am a potential ally, as far as you are concerned, Mr. Medina."

Medina approached the large window of his office. He remained behind the curtain, scanning the grounds of his mansion. He saw no one. No distant glint betrayed a telescope or a pair of binoculars.

Medina snarled into the phone.

"If this is some kind of joke...."

"Would I spend the time to hack through your fail safes to

call your personal phone merely to commit a prank?"

"Then what do you want?"

"I want to do you a favor."

Medina wondered at the metal voice. It sounded strangely crisp, unlike the usual muffle of a voice masking device. The vocal delivery was mechanical, but far superior to any computerized phone nonsense he had heard before.

"Well?" Medina asked.

"I have a means of," the voice paused, "removing the Alien from your concerns."

Medina laughed humorlessly.

"You make quite the claim. I might even go so far as to call it bragging."

"I do not brag."

"I have studied the Alien for years," Medina said. "I have never found a definitive way of 'removing him from my concerns.'"

"I assure you; I have the means."

"Then why don't you use them?"

"Discretion. I am not ready to play my hand. You, on the other hand, are dangerously close to being exposed."

"Is that a threat?"

"Mr. Medina, if I wanted you exposed, you'd already be in jail awaiting trial. It is a warning, not a threat. We both know the Alien will not let go the matter of the train explosion."

Medina agreed with the stranger, but said nothing. He paused in thought, trying to discern how his phone had been breached. How did this person know what they implied they knew about him?

"If my altruism isn't enough," the voice continued. "I can compensate you with a lucrative contract."

"A contract?"

"I need a special class of armaments. My investigations have shown only the Medina Corporation capable of building what I require."

"In exchange for what—incapacitating the Alien?" Medina asked. So far as he could tell, that was the best anyone could hope for. The Alien was invulnerable and invincible. Sometimes slowed, but never stopped.

"You have studied the Alien for years," the voice said. "Do you know the source of his superpowers?"

"Of course, that's no secret. He lived on a planet with higher gravity and a red sun. Earth's low gravity and yellow sun grant him superpower."

"We both know a cover story when we hear one." The voice nearly laughed, but for some odd reason Medina felt they could not. "A folk tale. A deflection from the truth. Since when does a spectrum of light give a being super powers?"

"Yes," Medina said, "I never quite believed it myself."

"I know the source of his power."

Medina stayed calm. He did not want to betray his mounting excitement to the mysterious caller. His hand tightened on the phone. His voice strained slightly through the tightness in his throat.

"You can cut him off from his power source?"

"No," the metallic voice confessed. "He is his own power source."

"What are you driving at?"

"Power sources can be overloaded."

Medina pursed his lips. Why had he never thought of it before? Rather than overcome the Alien's powers, he could attack them at the source. It was simple. He might be able to do it without the aid of the mysterious caller, but it would take time and research—time he did not have. His mysterious benefactor had already done the work—if he could be believed and trusted.

"Overload? And what will that do? Scramble his nervous system? Stun him? Put him in a coma for a week?"

A coma for a week would be a stretch. But Medina could do a lot in a week if he didn't need to worry about the Alien's interference.

"It will kill him, Mr. Medina." The voice was cold and calculating. "The overload will kill the Alien."

Kill the Alien? It didn't seem possible. It had never seemed possible. And yet, Medina's instinct told him he was not dealing with a liar.

Kill. Not incapacitate--kill. Assassinate the meddlesome

fool once and for all.

"Do we have an agreement, Mr. Medina?"

The conversation sounded too good to be true. It had to be a deal with the Devil—a deal between two devils. He couldn't entirely trust the devil on the other end, but Medina was confident he would come out on top as the bigger devil of the two.

"Go on," Medina said. "I'm listening."

4. DOWN AT THE DOCKS

If the situation with Medina hadn't distracted Dufresne, the mob boss might have paid more attention to the restaurant staff and gangsters milling around JACQUES'S BISTRO. He would not have recognized one of the staff at the restaurant. Jimmy Catalina had been a no-show and had sent his cousin, Fred Catalina, as a fill-in. Dufresne didn't know the guy well, but Fred looked enough like Jimmy to pass as Catalina's cousin—thanks to a partial disguise.

Fred knew everything he should have known, and the underlings weren't about to interrupt Dufresne's tense meal to ask for the boss's okay, so they confiscated his switchblade. Fred wasn't carrying a gun.

Fred cooked a tasty omelet, too. He fed some of the guys during Dufresne's meeting.

"Is that the guy?" Fred asked.

"What guy?"

"That rich one, from Pallas or something?"

Scottie-the head of Dufresne's security—turned a wary eye on Fred. The man was lean and tall, with a shock of unruly curls on top of his head, buzzed on the sides.

"Best stick to your omelets, Fred," Scottie said. "New guys shouldn't be asking questions. We've all got the dummy-up order: this lunch never happened."

"Of course, it never happened." Fred gave a rookie's nervous chuckle. He glanced around the hard faces in the kitchen. "That's why I'm cooking omelets for all of you—gotta get rid of the evidence."

After a moment, Scottie grinned and took a plate from Fred.

Fred let out a dramatic sigh, wiped sweat from his brow. It was a touch of overacting, but it appeared to go unnoticed.

Armed with nothing but his fists, Fred had shown his loyalty. He was the first to rush the dining room when the lunch between Dufresne and Medina had turned belligerent. After the incident had simmered down, he helped clean up. The others treated Fred like one of their own, asking about Jimmy and passing messages for him to get well. Some of them hoped Fred could stay around. Jimmy was no cook—most of them weren't.

Shanghaied into bar hopping after hours with his new friends, Fred was unable to extricate himself from the clingy web of Dufresne's organization until early evening.

He needed to visit Jimmy.

Jimmy lived in a rundown apartment building. He wasn't high up enough in the organization to afford a better place. He might have done better if he didn't spend so much on fancy cars that were always out of his price range.

Fred let himself into the apartment. The stale smell wafting from the empty pizza boxes in the kitchen gave off an unpleasant cheesy aroma. Fred walked past the chair where Jimmy sat and pulled open the windows.

"Air's foul in here, Jimmy," Fred said. He sniffed. "You need a bath, too."

Jimmy screamed at Fred. The gag in his mouth muffled the sound, but not the anger. Jimmy shuffled the chair a few inches forward, but after so much time, the bonds around his wrists and ankles had fatigued his limbs. He stopped moving.

"Calm down, Jimmy," Fred said. "I'm cutting you loose. But, first, there are a few ground rules we need to establish."

Jimmy said nothing, couldn't say anything. He glared. The glare didn't ruffle Fred's casual demeanor in the least.

"Jimmy, you work for Charles Dufresne. I was there with Mr. Dufresne today." Fred leaned over Jimmy's glowering face. "As close as this. Just think. I could have killed him."

Fred straightened up, paced in a circle around Jimmy's chair.

"Now, how do you think Mr. Dufresne is going to feel about you slacking on your job?"

Concern replaced a little of the anger Jimmy felt. He jerked his head, indicating Fred.

"Me?" Fred asked. Jimmy nodded vigorously. "Oh, you can tell him all about me. He might even believe you. But do you think that's going to save your skin? He'll string you up for falling down like this. Have you beaten within an inch of your life. Or kill you. I'm not sure which would be better. What do you think would be better?"

Jimmy neglected to respond.

"Now, that's the criminal side, Jimmy," Fred said. "Let's consider the law side. I know what you've done. Oh, it's all petty. Maybe you sell stolen pills and run some numbers. But if you were lazy and got picked up on an anonymous tip, and then Dufresne had to either deal with that or let you rot—you wouldn't come out ahead there, either."

Fred raised his hand, the slender form of a switchblade handle in his hand.

"So, here we are. You are Jimmy Catalina. I am Fred Catalina, your cousin. You've been sick, and you didn't want to disappoint the big boss man. You had me fill in today. You haven't seen me since. Trouble often comes calling for Fred Catalina. I'm probably lying low—someplace where I can cook some omelets."

Fred leaned over again, locked his eyes level with Jimmy's eyes.

"That's our story, cousin. Do you understand me?"

Jimmy Catalina nodded. He understood. The man—this "Fred"—was either clever or insane. Maybe both. It could all be bluff, but Jimmy wasn't ready to take a chance.

The switchblade clicked. Jimmy tensed, but instead of a slice or stab, his bonds jerked under the blade. Tingling sensations swarmed over his feet and hands. The return of feeling in his extremities was an excruciating relief.

Jimmy removed the gag. He almost screamed but thought better of it. He quietly cursed instead.

"You're some kind of an...." Jimmy's words stopped short.

The man was gone.

The door to Jimmy's apartment hung open. The screen in the open window had been raised. When had the guy done that? Jimmy wasn't sure which way the man had gone. Feet aching, rubbing his wrists and hands, Jimmy searched his apartment, the hallway, and the stairwell—but he couldn't stumble out into the street to give chase in his condition. He returned to his apartment and watched from his window for a long time, but the street remained quiet.

The madman had vanished.

The Moore-Rutledge observatory had been built southeast of Pallas, on the highest point available in the vicinity—Burke's Hill. The Alien could have flown, but instead drove his classic automobile sporting retro-futuristic fins and a convertible top. The car wasn't entirely classic—he had replaced the combustion engine with an electric one. Tech hidden behind the period-accurate glove compartment maintained contact with the Lair. The car climbed a ribbon of paved road spiraling up the hill to the observatory parking lot. The Robot sat in the passenger seat.

The observatory had experienced a break-in overnight. The Robot had considered the incident a petty crime and had let the information pass, choosing to continue to focus on Medina's network security. The Alien had pulled out more data and files from the usual electronic noise. By the time he finished, the Alien had been eager to head to the observatory.

"Again, I must query," the Robot said. They walked past the entrance sign and followed the concrete slat walkway. "Would our time be better spent attempting to secure evidence against Milton Medina for his part in the train wreck?"

"Crime fighting is multitasking in the field as well as from within the Lair," the Alien said. "If we serially focused on one situation at a time, we would not make much headway. We have all the evidence we are going to get against Medina—which is nothing right now. While we wait for something, we will investigate here."

"A simple breaking and entering. Surely, the police do not need your assistance for something so routine."

"Simple? Yes. Routine? Anything but. That is what attracted me to investigate."

"Why do you believe this is not routine?"

"Breaking and entering are usually accompanied by theft— or violence. Neither occurred in this case."

"Then I would surmise the perpetrators were scared away before either could be committed," the Robot said.

"The alarms were disabled. There were no staff in the building at the time. The criminals broke in, spent an unknown amount of time in the facility, and then left of their own accord."

Normally open to the public, the observatory had been closed for the day in the wake of the crime. A man in a white smock and stylish leather dress shoes met them at the entrance. He wore large framed glasses, and his full beard and receding hair grew in curls, giving him a frazzled appearance. He smiled as he held open the glass door.

"Pleasure to see you!"

"And you, Professor Vaughan," the Alien replied.

Vaughan gazed at the Robot.

"And this is?"

"I am the Robot."

The professor turned to the Alien. "That's new."

"No, it isn't. First time doing field work. I might let you see a schematic."

The professor's eyes went wide. "Would you?"

"Certainly. But some other time."

"I thought your discipline was astrophysics, Professor," said the Robot.

"Oh. It is. But you know us scientists—dabblers all." Vaughan continued to circle the Robot, sometimes leaning in for a closer look, other moments rearing back to observe the entire construction from head to feet. "Engineering, robotics, computers—much like yourselves, I'm certain."

The astrophysicist tore his attention away from the Robot.

"On this fine sunny afternoon, I must conclude you have not stopped by to stargaze," Vaughan said.

"Correct," the Robot said. "We are here to investigate last night's break-in."

"Oh, you heard about that. What am I saying? Of course, you did!"

Vaughan bustled along the main corridor, and they followed in his wake. They entered the rotunda where the telescope waited for evening beneath the closed dome roof.

The professor spread his arms wide and spun in a circle.

"The extent of the robbery. Not even a pen missing."

"No vandalism?" the Alien asked. "No destruction of property?"

"None."

"If someone breaks in and steals nothing, and they are not lying in wait to attack someone, we might assume two things," the Alien said.

"Those are?" asked the professor.

"They came to leave something behind. Or," the Alien gazed up at the industrial sized telescope jutted over their heads, "they wanted something that could not be stolen. Which means they would have used the telescope in situ."

Vaughan face went slack.

"I hadn't even thought of that!"

The astrophysicist ran up the stairs to the controller seat beneath the telescope. He typed on a computer situated to the left of the controls.

The Robot and the Alien turned around at the whine and flutter of an old, dot matrix printer as it spewed out a steady stream of paper.

"It seems Professor Vaughan enjoys a mix of equipment as much as you do," the Robot said.

The printing halted. The Alien ripped the final page away from the printer and scooped up the paper stack. He rapidly flipped through the pages.

"This log has been altered. An entire twenty minutes is missing from last night."

Behind them, Vaughan raced back down the steps to join them.

"So, there was vandalism."

"Not vandalism." The Alien studied the log lines on the printout. "Someone covered their tracks."

"Someone broke in to use the telescope?" Vaughan asked.

"It appears so."

"To what end? They could have booked the time."

"They didn't want it known. They wanted to observe the skies in secret."

"Whatever for?" Vaughan asked.

"I don't know. Other than a range of coordinates and the time frame of twenty minutes, we don't know what they were searching for."

"We can scan that area tonight, if you'd like," the Professor offered.

The Alien shook his head.

"There is no guarantee the final coordinate was where they looked. If they were smart, they would have entered the final coordinates as random. I would not underestimate the intelligence of someone who can disarm your system and operate a state-of-the-art telescope. I am certain they would have covered their tracks."

"What does it mean?" the astrophysicist asked. "Do we need a security guard now?"

"I wouldn't worry too much about it, Professor." The Alien crossed his arms and knit his green brow. "Be vigilant. Upgrade the alarm."

"I will," the professor said.

They bade farewell and returned to the Alien's automobile. He opened the driver's side door, paused, and looked back at the observatory.

"What is wrong?" the Robot asked.

"Nothing."

"Your facial expression implies otherwise."

The Alien sighed and let his shoulders slump.

"This incident feels more...." the Alien searched for the word. He straightened up quickly as if a thought had occurred to him. He gently shook his head. "I can't quite put my finger on it—as the humans say. This little crime feels like something more ominous than innocuous."

The Understudy scanned the dock warehouse through the green haze of night vision. Two bruisers waited at the loading door. A car pulled along the pier, headlights washing out her view of the scene. The docks of Crowsport were a nest of illegal activities. She had done stakeouts here before, but there was something special about tonight's mission. She just didn't know what the mission was, exactly.

The Protector pulled the small, powerful night-vision binoculars from her hand. They disappeared into one of the large pockets of his leather trench coat. The coat's pockets never gave the appearance of bulging, but they should have, given the number of gadgets they carried. The upturned collar, oversized like the coat's pockets, might lead one to believe the coat itself was too large, but it fit him neatly. His fedora—which never seemed to dislodge in the heat of action—had a slightly oversized brim, which shaded his face even in good light.

"Why don't we get night vision goggles?" the Understudy asked. She was young, in her early twenties. Her shoulder length brown hair fanned out from under an aviator's cap. Goggles were perched on her forehead. Tinted, they served as a mask as well as eye protection. She favored the same drab leather as her mentor. The browns and blacks helped blend into the evening shadows of Crowsport.

She shifted her legs to avoid the sensation of pins and needles in her feet. The duo had been crouched behind a rack of pipes for too long, and she wanted to spring into action. Boredom had set in.

"Still have spots in your eyes from those headlights?"

"Yeah." She rubbed her eyes, knowing the gesture was futile.

"That's why. Try an operation with night vision goggles and someone flips a light switch." The Protector flicked out his fingers. "Flash! You're blind as a bat. Quite the disadvantage."

The Protector tapped his pockets, mumbling words. The Understudy knew he recited a litany of the contents of each pocket. A complete inventory in his head, constantly rehearsed.

"You need to learn to operate in the dark."

"Oh, the jokes I could make," the Understudy said. "Speaking of working in the dark, now will you tell me why we're here?"

"No," the Protector said. "You'll deduce that yourself. Who owns this place?"

"Letters on the side of the building would indicate TYLER IMPORT EXPORT."

"But we know that's a front. Do you remember what I said earlier?"

"The paper trail leads to Dufresne, the mobster."

"A legal laundering business which can double for illegal when smuggling is involved."

"We're here to bust Dufresne?" The Understudy wrinkled her face. "The police must know about this already."

"Dufresne's managed to keep them looking the other way," the Protector said. Bribery among police, politicians, and criminals was all too common in Crowsport. Corruption was one of many fronts in the battle against crime. "Maybe we can stir up enough of a hornets' nest to force them to act against Dufresne. But that's not our primary goal tonight."

"What is our goal?"

"Let's say you're a mobster. You smuggle goods. There's an accident. People saw the illegal cargo on your transport."

"Fell off the truck?"

"Something like that."

"Then you rub out the ones who saw the illegal cargo," the Understudy said.

"Harsh."

"I was thinking like a gangster."

"Fair enough," said the Protector. "But what if it's nearly impossible to kill that person?"

"Impossible to kill?" The Understudy considered for a moment. "Someone unreachable?"

"No," the Protector said. "Someone impervious."

"Impervious?" The Understudy's eyes went wide. "The Alien? The Alien. The train crash!"

The Protector nodded and flashed a small smile of satisfaction. He seemed pleased with her quick deduction. "Dufresne can't kill the Alien. Instead, he'll do whatever he can to cover his tracks."

The Understudy snapped her fingers. "The shipment on

the wrecked train wasn't the first. Whatever the cargo from Pallas was, there might already be previous shipments in the warehouse."

"Bingo!" The Protector nodded. "And they need to move it—fast."

"How do you know all this?"

"Two parts deduction, one part field work." The Protector grinned. "Have I ever told you about my cousin, Jimmy Catalina?"

"No."

"Never mind. We have company."

Three vehicles entered the wharf—two small trucks and a shipping company van. A rotund man in a loose-fitting gray suit stepped out from the awaiting automobile. Cocked on his head sat a fedora two sizes too small, and a pencil mustache etched from his lips and down to his chin.

"That's Dufresne," the Protector said. "Overseeing the operation, personally. It must be a big deal—as I thought."

A loaded forklift emerged from the warehouse, rectangular wooden crates stacked on its fork. Each crate was simple, unmarked, a meter long and perhaps thirty centimeters wide. The men started loading the crates into the trucks.

The cargo appeared lightweight, as each man was able to carry a crate with no assistance from others.

"Not very heavy," the Understudy said. "Guns?"

"Guns didn't blow up that train," the Protector said. "If those are explosives, they must be advanced to weigh so little and cause so much damage. The list of suspects narrows."

The Understudy suspected the Protector had already reduced the list before making his observation.

"So. We're going to stop them?"

"I'm not sure we can." The Protector pointed toward the docks. "But if we can get ahold of a crate or two…."

"We can get some evidence."

"Yes. Dufresne isn't the top dog in this case. He's just a contractor moving the goods."

"Do you know who the top dog is?"

"I have my suspicions," the Protector said. "Which is why I

want evidence to back them up."

Loud engines trundled in the water. Three double-decker pontoon boats sidled along the pier. Each boat had a pilot, plus one or two armed men on the upper deck. The armed men climbed down, and dock workers carried crates to the waiting boats, passing the lightweight deliveries over the gunwales. They stacked the crates on the open bottom decks of the boats.

"He's splitting the cargo."

"Or he's cleverer than I thought," the Protector said. He shook his head slightly. "Maybe they're creating a feint. The trucks could be a decoy."

"Or the boats," the Understudy said. "All by land or all by sea?"

"Maybe a mix," the Protector said. "A couple of trucks, one or two boats carrying empty loads."

"We split up then."

"No."

"I'm ready!"

"No."

"It's the only decent chance of getting ahold of something!" The Understudy folded her arms in anger and frustration.

The Understudy couldn't tell whether the Protector's hesitation was a concern for the success of the mission, or fear for her. This could be the first time he cut her loose, the first time she fought on her own instead of punching and kicking at his side.

The Protector let out a sigh.

"Grab and go. We don't need to destroy the cargo or take them down. Grab a crate, move. If it's too heavy, get it open and take a sample."

The Protector pulled a device from his pocket. It was the size and shape of an old-fashioned Derringer pistol. The Understudy pulled her goggles down.

They broke from cover, the Protector fired as they ran.

The projectiles were no bigger than grapes. On impact, they produced a voluminous smoke screen. When the duo reached the docks, the men were calling out in confusion, ordering each other not to shoot for fear of crossfire.

"Stay exactly where you are!" Dufresne yelled. "Watch your blind spots! No one is shooting at us yet!"

The Understudy moved through the smoke. She ran, navigating by sound and an image she had committed to memory before the smokescreen had been laid down. There would be a man to her right. He was there, a dark shape looming in the gray smoke. With a low, sweeping kick, she sent him toppling to the ground.

"Get the boats out!" someone shouted.

Engines revved and propellers churned in the water.

She heard a holler and a thud of a body hitting the ground followed by a wheeze of someone who had their wind knocked out. There was a metallic click of a released catch and a whirling, twirling buzz. Another body thudded to the ground. The Protector had attacked his prey, too.

When the smoke swallowed the Understudy, the Protector felt his heart rate increase, but he pushed all doubt away. The Understudy had trained. Ready or not, the moment was upon them both. Worry and distraction could be fatal.

He heard a thump in the smoke.

"Oof!" someone gasped.

The Protector grinned. His protege would do fine.

Three precise blows knocked his first target senseless, and the man fell to the ground. The Protector peered into the smoke, willing for a sight of his second target. He couldn't see the man exactly, but he had an idea where to look. He had memorized the men's positions and kept a mental image of the scene in his mind. He hoped the Understudy remembered to use the technique, too.

As soon as he could discern movement in the haze, he drew his bolo tube from his spacious trench coat pocket. He pressed the button. The whirling balls, joined by a cord, arched across the space, caught someone around the ankles and calves. The criminal toppled over in surprise; his gun clattered across the pier.

The Protector heard feet running away. They weren't loud or large. He knew the gait and quick stride of his apprentice.

The men they were fighting were all taller or larger than she was.

She was heading toward the water.

The Protector headed toward the trucks.

The Understudy's second target had dropped to his knee, waiting to trip her. She espied the hunched shape and kept running toward him, leaping over him at the last moment. She spun and landed a roundhouse kick against his chest as he stood up.

This brawler was tougher than her last takedown. He kept his feet firmly planted. He didn't deflect the blow, he absorbed it. He punched a meaty fist at her, but she spun into the smoke and disappeared from his view. She sidestepped, and the man predictably moved in a straight line after her. She went for another kick, but halted. Her mission wasn't to take everyone down. She needed evidence. She padded away deeper into the smoke.

The smoke dispersed to wisps and tendrils as the Understudy reached the edge of the smokescreen near the pier and boats. Two of the boats had already accelerated away out of range. The remaining had trouble. The motor raced. Either something was amiss, or the pilot had flooded the engine in a panic.

She raced toward the boat and stopped halfway. From the deck, multiple gun barrels pointed in her direction.

The Protector swung at a shape in the dark. The shape leapt back far enough to raise a sawed-off shotgun. The gangster hesitated.

The Protector whirled. Another creep was charging him, a vague shape, and he caught the glint of a knife. The shotgun man understood a blast from his weapon would spray pellets too wide and might catch his associate with friendly fire. The Protector's empty bolo tube expanded into a riot baton with a flick of his arm. He spun widdershins once, catching the knife man on the shoulder, and then reversed, striking the side of the man's head. The knife man collapsed.

The Protector spun to his left as the shotgun roared. Before the next shot, he crouched to one knee. Singlehanded, he flung three small throwing knives in a cluster. Two stuck in the man's shoulder, his trigger arm went limp. The third blade grazed the tough's ear.

The knives weren't fatal, but they served as harassment and distraction. The Protector closed the distance and pummeled the man, striking sharp jabs to the abdomen and head. The man sprawled to the ground, senseless.

The Protector heard boat engines roaring to life. He'd been disoriented and arrived closer to the water than to the warehouse and the ground transportation.

He wondered if the Understudy would do something foolish. He had taken down the three men from the first truck, so the vehicle wasn't going anywhere for a few moments.

Just a peek would do.

The Understudy thought she was dead. She and the Protector had been in scrapes before. There had been guns a few times, but she couldn't recall if she'd ever been shot at. There had been punches and kicks and knives and clubs. Had she ever heard the crack of a gun?

The men aiming their guns at her were not fooling around. She read the deadly intent in their faces.

At the smoke's edge, the Protector appeared.

"Eff bee!" he yelled.

Eff bee.

F-B.

Code.

The Understudy turned her head and covered her ears as she threw herself to the ground. A flash-bang grenade detonated in midair, temporarily blinding the men on the boat. They fired, and bullets flew wildly.

"Get 'em!" The Protector said. He disappeared back into the smoke, which was rapidly dissipating.

The Understudy scrambled to her feet, hoping she looked more impressive and graceful than she felt. She ran for the boat.

She took a running leap off the pier. The pilot fumbled the throttle. The boat churned away from the pier, its motion disrupting her landing. She landed on the deck, her foot twisted, and she went down. The crew were recovering from the flash-bang. They shook their heads, shoved fingers in their ears, and rubbed their eyes.

One ruffian stood with a hand on the rail. She spotted a boat hook on her left, yanked it free. A solid poke in the stomach sent the man over the rail and into the water. She hoped he could swim. She didn't want a drowning on her conscience.

One down, two to go.

She would leave the pilot for last. She would need to take him down carefully. She might lose control of the boat if she wasn't cautious.

The Protector circled back through the dissipating smoke. The Understudy had a chance of capturing the boat. He would attend to the trucks.

With the smoke cover fading, friendly fire was no longer a concern to the gangsters. Their guns blazed. The Protector dove for cover behind a stack of lumber. He heard harsh tones of loudly whispered orders. He had noticed in his crime-fighting career that unless the men were ex-military, it never occurred to them to learn basic hand signals. The Protector wasn't about to complain about the gangsters' lack of innovation.

He hurled his last flash-bang and dashed across the open through the half-open warehouse doors. No gangsters were in there, but the crates had been cleared, too. All the cargo had been transferred to the pier or loaded into the vehicles.

Two men, blinking and shaking off the after-effects of the grenade, covered the front of the warehouse with their guns. The Protector could not emerge without being seen.

Dufresne harangued his remaining goons loading the last crates onto the vehicles, then hopped in the backseat of his car, which sped off. The two trucks pulled away moments later. The rear doors of the oversized shipping company van hung open.

"Come on!" someone called from the back of the van to the two guards.

One man turned and dashed toward the van. The other one ran clumsily backwards, keeping the warehouse doors covered.

The Protector preferred his grappling gun for climbing, but

it had other uses. He rolled across the open space between the doors of the warehouse, came up on a kneeling position, and fired. The hook grazed the facing man's head, forcing him to duck. Through the remaining open door at the back of the van, the hook punched slightly into the wood of a crate. The Protector thumbed a remote in his pocket, and micro-explosives built into the hook tips drove them deeper into the wood. The fleeing van kept moving, and the crate toppled out of the open van door.

But not before a flash and stream of smoke emerged from the darker recess of the van.

The Protector leapt to the left. The RPG exploded against the right front interior wall of the warehouse. The shockwave knocked him off his feet. Dazed and sprawled on the floor, he took a moment to recover. He felt heat and inhaled smoke. The warehouse was ablaze.

The Protector crawled toward the open doors, ignoring his pain. He hoped the structural integrity of the building would hold long enough for him to escape.

A pistol popped. The boat rolled, and despite the close quarters, the shot missed. The young shooter looked alarmed. He stared at the pistol and seemed shocked he had pulled the trigger. The Understudy launched off her good leg and tackled him. She grabbed for his wrist and beat his hand against the rail. He lost his grip on the pistol. The gun bounced twice on the deck and spun over the edge of the boat into the bay.

The Understudy stepped back, sucked in air. Her opponent came at her. She executed a judo throw and sent the bruiser into the water after his pistol.

Somewhere in the distance behind the boat, something exploded. The sky lit up and flashed orange. She was too busy to turn her attention. Her ankle throbbed. She lifted herself up and limped toward the ship's wheel.

The pilot saw her coming, pushed the throttle to full. The boat lurched. The Understudy flailed her arms, trying to stay upright. The pilot took his chance and leapt into the water.

They were gone! She had the boat!

The Understudy's relief evaporated into brief panic. The

boat careened toward a buoy. The pilot had done his best to destroy the evidence.

Preservation instinct spurred her to run for the wheel. The effort was a complete failure. The shaking boat, her bad ankle, and the wet deck conspired against her. She fell. Panic threatened to paralyze her into inaction as did the hypnotic flashing of the buoy's lights. Blue. Green. Blue. Green.

Maybe the pain in her leg was worse than she thought. Shock? Shouldn't she be saving her life?

The Understudy let out a scream of terror, fear, and pain. She lugged her body upright, threw herself bodily across the gap to the pilot's seat. She hauled back the throttle, but the deceleration wasn't enough. She cranked the wheel. The boat curved through the water. The buoyant pontoons prevented the boat from going over, but the left pontoon ripped against the side of the buoy.

She adjusted the throttle to a manageable speed. The torn pontoon was filling with water. The boat crawled along. Wincing at her sore ankle and gasping as her breathing returned to normal, she turned the boat back toward the burning docks.

Fire engulfed the warehouse.

There were three crates on board. Keeping an eye on her heading, she opened the crates using her multi-tool. They were empty.

"All that for nothing!"

She let the boat putter its way back to the docks, growing more impatient as the fire spread. Her ankle throbbed.

The Protector waited for her at the edge of a pier, a smashed crate perched on his shoulder. The flames blazed behind him, orange and yellow licking against the dark night.

"All I got were dummies." The Understudy pointed at the Protector's crate. "Is that a genuine article?"

The Protector nodded.

"They don't weigh much, but they pack a wallop." He climbed aboard as police and fire sirens grew louder.

"You look hurt," he said.

"I am. Twisted my ankle."

He looked over the side of the boat, observed the flooded pontoon and frowned.

"We won't be escaping by sea."

"Escaping?"

"Big mess. I don't have the best relationship with the police."

"I wonder why?"

"I am working on that. Public relations and what-not."

He knelt and tested her ankle with a few light pokes and gentle squeezes. She winced and gasped a few times.

"Nothing broken, but you're going to have a rough walk home."

From his pocket, he pulled out two short lengths of hard plastic and an athletic bandage. He handed them to the Understudy.

"Do your best." The Protector moved to the pilot station. "I'll try to get us a few docks down the coast before we need to get back on dry land."

The Understudy remembered her medic training. Wrapping her own ankle was awkward, though.

The Protector navigated the lop-sided boat through the dark bay. The police cars, fire trucks, ambulances, and a harbor patrol boat were arriving at the scene of the conflagration. The Understudy heard helicopters in the distance, too.

"Time to be gone," the Protector said.

He clambered out, tied off the boat, and helped the Understudy climb up to the pier. He offered his arm. Her splint worked, but she took his offer and leaned on him.

Together, they disappeared into the shadows of Crowsport.

5. THE TRAP

For the third night in a row, the Alien and the Robot hid in darkness under thick pine trees. They kept watch on one of Medina's factories. A perimeter fence surrounded the property. Whether the duo was surveying the production of household appliances or a run of armaments had yet to determined. The billionaire's factories were modular and could be refitted to produce many items.

A few nighttime lights stayed on, but the building was closed for business after eleven thirty in the evening. There were no third-shift workers. If there were automated systems or industrial robots toiling on the inside, no sounds escaped.

"If I could get in there...." The Alien sat in a lotus position on a bed of pine needles.

"That would be breaking and entering," the Robot said.

"Yes, it would be," someone said in a hushed voice. "We do it all the time."

The Robot turned. A man and a woman emerged from the shadows.

"I did not detect you there."

"No, but he did."

The man pointed at the Alien, who continued keeping wary eyes on the factory. The duo's arrival had not surprised him.

"Though, I suspect," the man continued, "he heard us more than anything else."

The Alien raised his eyebrows briefly.

"Robot," the Alien said. "You have not met, but I think you can deduce who these people are."

The man wore a fedora hat and trench coat. The young

woman wore a leather aviator cap and goggles.

"The Protector and his protégé, the Understudy."

"At your service," the young woman said.

"What brings you to Pallas?" the Alien asked.

"Undoubtedly, the same thing that brings you out at night," the Protector said. "Shadows and darkness are my thing. I thought you preferred working in the daytime."

"I work whenever it is required."

"I bet you don't need sleep, either," the Understudy commented. "Lucky."

Without waiting for an invitation, the Protector crouched beside the Alien.

"I've got something for you."

"Oh?"

"It's a little too bulky for stealth," the Understudy said. "We left it back in the car."

"It'll save you getting in trouble. It's one of Medina's toys. A hand-held missile."

The Alien turned and scrutinized the Protector's face.

"I knew that would get your attention." The Protector grinned. He pointed across the way at the building. "Why don't you just take a peek with your x-ray vision?"

"There are strips and grids of lead worked throughout the factory walls. I can only see bits and pieces. I almost believe Medina is teasing me."

"Teasing you?"

"Why not put up complete sheets of lead to cover the walls entirely?"

"Maybe the additions were rushed as a temporary measure since your interview with him," the Robot said.

"Possible."

"Interview?" The Protector laughed. "You are direct, aren't you?"

The Alien said nothing.

The four lapsed into silence, monitoring the building.

The Understudy stood beside the Robot. She put out her hand. The Robot stared at the offered extremity.

"Shake?" The Understudy smiled. "Nice to meet you?"

"Ah," the Robot said. It raised its hand and clasped hers.

"I'm glad you have fine control over your hydraulics—or whatever engineering makes your body move."

"Indeed. I could crush your hand easily."

The Understudy withdrew her hand with a yank.

"I'm surprised to see you here." She indicated the Protector with a nod of her head. "He's mentioned you, of course. I was expecting…well, I don't know what I was expecting."

"You probably weren't expecting me here. Out doing field work."

"That's true. Seemed to me you were a part of the famous Alien's lair."

"A part of it?"

"Sure. Like some super mechanical genius spider at the heart of a tech web with all these wires running in and out of you."

The Robot cocked its head quizzically.

"I never gave her that impression," the Protector said. "I said you never leave the Lair. Or, you never did before. The rest is just her imagination."

The Protector directed a question to the Alien.

"Are you thinking or brooding?"

"Why would I brood?"

"You're frustrated with Medina. There are still many crimes to fight—even in Pallas, even after your crusade. Why obsess on him?"

"Obsess is a strong word." The Alien shrugged and sighed. "There are men who believe their wealth puts them above the law. Money does not make a person exempt."

"Medina doesn't believe his wealth exempts him," the Protector said. "But he has enough hubris to believe he has a certain superiority. He believes his superiority somehow makes him exempt."

"You've kept tabs on him?"

"I know his ilk—all too well."

"Did you know he's missing a laser?"

"No."

"There is another thing," the Alien hesitated, then

continued, "Did you know someone broke into the Moore-Rutledge observatory?"

"No. What's to steal?" the Protector asked.

"Precisely. Nothing. Whoever broke in used the telescope and then erased the log."

The Protector rubbed his chin.

"Peculiar."

"At the least," the Alien agreed. "I can't help feeling it's something bigger than it appears."

A persistent beeping noise sounded. In the quiet night it sounded like a klaxon. The Protector and the Understudy turned on the Robot. The Alien leapt to his feet.

"What is that?" the Alien asked.

"Something I've been waiting for," said the Robot.

The Protector shushed. "Turn it off before we're lit up like a Christmas tree out here. They must have spotlights."

The Robot touched his arm and the beeping halted. A tablet telescoped out from the Robot's forearm and displayed a stream of code scrolling up the screen.

"We're in," the Robot reported. "I considered that this factory's security system might be easier to penetrate than M. M. Labs."

"Why did you think that?" the Understudy asked.

The Robot shrugged.

"M. M. Labs are the brains—the research, the designs, the sensitive data. A factory floor, though dealing with proprietary material, would perhaps have slightly more relaxed security protocols."

"Almost sounds like you had a hunch," the Protector said.

"That is not possible."

"You did this on your own?" the Alien asked.

The Robot nodded.

The Protector turned to the Alien.

"See?" He pointed a thumb at the Robot. "Now the Robot is obsessed, too."

The Alien studied the tablet screen.

"Can it be traced?"

"No. It's an algorithm and programming from my own... brain. It's like I'm in there."

"How deep?"

"Not very."

"Does the code tell us anything?" the Understudy asked.

"No," the Robot replied. "But I have access to the cameras."

A grid of black and white camera feeds appeared in the center of the screen. There were two wide shots of a factory floor, the machinery inactive. Another view covered the entrance driveway. Still more images flashed around the perimeter fence of the complex. Three of the stairwells were void of any activity.

Dark shapes and shadows flitted down the fourth staircase.

The Robot zoomed the camera and heightened the resolution.

A group clad in baggy black clothes and black ski masks exited the stairwell door. They carried pistols on their hips. One or two also slung heavier weapons across their backs.

The men—or men and women, the clothing obscured features—pulled the tarp off a pallet of small crates. One operative secured a forklift and moved a smaller pallet beside the larger one. The intruders hurriedly transferred a portion of the goods.

"Another robbery."

"It has to be an inside job, or the security alarms would be tripped," the Alien said. "I'm surprised they would dare it twice."

"I'm surprised Medina hadn't already tracked down the perpetrators," the Understudy said.

"I wonder." The Alien pursed his lips, tapped them with his forefinger. "Did you finally crack his security, or did he let you in?"

"Why would he 'let me in'?"

"It's too good to be true." The Alien shook his head. "Convenient. Just the excuse I'd been waiting for."

"If Medina wanted you to prevent a theft, he could have called you," the Protector said.

"This looks better. More enticing. Not incriminating. He knows I won't let those missiles fall into the hands of terrorists."

"You believe it is a trap," said the Robot.

"Yes. I'm ninety-five percent certain."

"I calculate the possibility of a trap at ninety-seven-point three percent."

"A trap which can also be an opportunity."

"To survey the interior of the facility while we are preventing the crime."

"Exactly."

"What about the trap?" the Understudy asked.

"Whatever it might be, I doubt it is as foolproof as Medina would like to believe." The Alien crossed his arms over his chest. "I am not a person he can put in a cage—or shoot down."

"All right," said the Protector. "Wait here."

"What?" The Alien raised an eyebrow.

"You're not inconspicuous. And the shiny ebony robot with red highlights might be a giveaway, too." He nodded at the Understudy. "Let us spring the trap. Medina won't expect that."

The Alien gave curt nod, frustration etched on his face.

"If there's trouble you can't handle, we're coming in after you."

The fence wasn't electrified. The only measure of security was barbed wire looping along the top. The Protector and the Understudy scaled the obstacle. Reaching the top, the Protector pulled a pair of wire cutters from a pocket. After a few strategic snips, a length of barbed wire dangled away. They pulled themselves over and dropped into the compound.

The Understudy moved forward. The Protector halted her with an outstretched arm.

"This is too easy. Why don't we see lights inside the building? They'd need flashlights."

"Night vision goggles," said the Understudy.

"I couldn't tell from that low-res video. Ssh." He put fingers to his lips. "For that matter, I don't hear anything."

"They're stealing weapons, not marching a parade out the front door."

"Certainly not the front door. Where and how are they planning to get out?"

The Understudy shrugged. She hadn't considered what plan the robbers might have.

"Let's get a closer look."

The Protector shook his head, but said, "All right."

The Alien watched the video of the robbery in progress. He clutched the Robot's arm. On the screen, the group had halted their clandestine labor and darted toward the door to the stairs.

"Why are they back in the stairwell? Are they coming up?" the Alien wondered. "Did those two trip a silent alarm?"

The shadowy men seemed to reconsider their intent. They paused on the first landing, flashed hand signals. The video glitched and then showed the group descending the stairs again.

In the same order and manner they had originally.

"Oh no," said the Alien.

"It's a plant, a video loop," the Robot confirmed. "There is no one in the building. Or, perhaps they are waiting—masked by the video overlay."

The Understudy followed the Protector. They dashed toward the building. As the duo passed over a large in-ground hatch, the heavy metal door flew open. They were hurled into the air, arms and legs flailing. They hit the ground with grunts and cries of surprise. They rolled, used the momentum to avoid a more damaging impact.

An alarm sounded. The Understudy whirled, expecting the building to light up and armed men to swarm out.

The building remained quiet.

The alarm grew louder. Ignoring the dull throb of pain in her body, she focused her attention. She located the source as coming from the open hatch. Beside her, the Protector grunted.

Something was coming up from the hatchway.

Red and blue lights flashed from the top of the oversized mechanical head. A speaker grille formed a mouth from which the alarm continued to squawk. The machine continued to rise, riding on a lift platform.

The Protector, still on his back and propped on his elbows, gazed up at the looming form.

The large automaton--four times larger than the

Robot—cocked its head and gazed downward. It looked like a centaur—a humanoid, square bulky upper body attached to a four-legged torso. The legs appeared spindly, but when the robotic monstrosity stepped off the platform and walked toward them, it moved with balance—if not smoothness and grace.

The alarm stopped. A grating mechanical voice boomed.

"Intruders."

"This probably isn't good," the Protector said.

The centaur-bot pointed its arms at the Protector and the Understudy. Where there would have been hands and fingers, three pincers protruded from each limb. The digits shot out from their appendages, each attached by an artificial sinewy cable.

The mechanical tentacles grabbed for the hapless duo.

The Alien did not hesitate. He flew in a blur over the fence. Even at accelerated speed, he did not have time to rescue both the Protector and the Understudy. He interposed his body between the lashing tentacles and the Understudy. The cables entwined his body and retracted into the left robotic arm. The right arm had snagged the Protector.

Below, he saw the Robot fly over the fence. The Robot helped the Understudy to her feet. They both turned their faces upward.

"Friend of yours?" the Protector asked the Robot. He was gasping for air. The cables had a crushing strength. If they were designed to hold the Alien, the machine wouldn't understand it was killing the Protector with the same strength of grip.

The Alien strained against the cables. They were surprisingly resilient. He would snap them eventually, but it would take longer than a simple breaking of rope or the effort of breaking a chain. The extra few moments could be costly.

"I'm surprised he hasn't snapped those cables," the Robot commented.

"I'm not."

The Robot's face had no expression, but it titled its head slightly, a quizzical gesture it had learned from humans.

"If someone set a trap for the Alien, they weren't going to

use fishing line." The Understudy lowered her goggles over her eyes. "I know the Alien is super-strong and impervious to bullets and what-not. Would acid hurt him?"

"I believe not."

"Good." She pulled a vial from her utility belt. "I won't need to be accurate. Fly me as near to the arm as you can."

The Robot slipped his arms under the Understudy's armpits and launched. The security robot's large head tracked their movement.

"Intruders," the grating voice said, "in restricted, private airspace of Medina Incorporated."

"I don't think he knows what to make of us," the Understudy said.

They flew over and then swooped down at the left arm. The centaur-bot's right appendage swatted at them. The Protector appeared worse for the wear with each jostle. The Understudy primed the mini-explosive charge and tossed the vial. It burst on the tentacles wrapping the Alien's chest.

The Robot twisted in flight, absorbing a blow from the gigantic right arm. They cartwheeled through the air. The Understudy felt butterflies in her stomach, and she knew they were falling. She imagined the weight of the Robot crushing her into the ground on impact.

It wasn't a pleasant image.

The Alien burst his bonds. Bits of cable and mechanical pincer snapped into the air. He faced a split-second decision: free the Protector, or stop the plummeting Understudy and the Robot.

The Alien risked that the Robot would course correct before they smashed into the ground. He hoped he was right.

He zipped over. The Protector had gone limp. The Alien pulled against the cables, bracing his feet against the arm. If he couldn't break them, he could relieve the pressure on the Protector's diaphragm, at least.

The cables eased off and then tore away. The unexpected release sent the Alien flying, and the Protector fell.

The Robot regained enough control to roll its body toward the ground. It was a noble gesture, but the Understudy figured she would still break plenty of bones impacting the hard casing of the Robot's body. She closed her eyes, wincing in anticipation of pain.

She heard a roar, a *fwoomp* sound, and felt a surge of heat around her feet. The wind increased around her face, jostling the curls of hair poking out from under her aviator's cap. She opened one eye, and saw the ground blur past, only two feet below the Robot. She craned her neck and saw an orange-red glow burning outward in a cone from beneath the soles of the Robot's feet.

"Rocket boots?"

"In a sense, though I have no boots," the Robot said

"Why rockets if you can defy gravity?"

"Maneuverability, as I just demonstrated," the Robot said. "I lack the dexterity of the Alien."

The rockets stopped flaring. The Robot swung into the air in an arc and landed smoothly on its feet.

The Protector fired his grappling pistol. Its hook slipped into the crevice of the centaur-bot's bent elbow. It wouldn't hold long against the composite material of the guardian's outer casing. The Protector pulled the line taut and swung his body under the robotic arm. The leverage helped stabilize the line briefly enough for him to slide down to a safe distance above the ground. He let go of the line and landed in a crouch.

The Alien arrived at his side a moment later.

"I thought it had crushed the wind out of you—maybe killed you."

"I played dead; it eased its squeeze—like a python."

"Do pythons do that?"

The Protector shrugged.

"Maybe? It was the only move I had." The Protector put a hand over his side. "My ribs barely held out without cracking; I'll be black-and-blue all over."

The Robot and the Understudy ran to them. The giant mechanical centaur-bot regarded the intruders, calculating its next move. It would not wait long.

"Can you give it a good sock in the mouth?" the Protector asked the Alien.

"I can smash it to bits—eventually. Medina has concocted some new polymer, mixed it with its metal casing. It won't be a quick job."

"I bet he put just enough lead in the mix so you can't examine its guts for weaknesses."

"Correct."

"Can you get any deeper into Medina's network?" The Understudy asked the Robot. "Find schematics of the thing?"

"My penetration of Medina's security was a feint."

"Try again!"

The Robot fell silent as though listening for voices in the ether.

"I cannot. I have lost communication with our central computer," the Robot said.

"Wireless services." The Understudy rolled her eyes.

"We have our own wireless and our own power source at the Lair. There is nothing wrong with my transmitter." The Robot turned to the Alien. "Someone must have penetrated the penthouse."

"Impossible. Even so, the alarms would have alerted us."

"Alarms can be bypassed," the Protector said. "You've been setup."

"Stay here!" The Alien leapt into the sky.

"Wait!"

The Protector's appeal fell on deaf ears. Already the Alien was a receding blue and green blur.

"We need to get after him. This feels more like a setup than a distraction." The Protector turned to the Robot. "Can you fly?"

"I have anti-gravity capability, but I do not match his speed."

"You'll still make better time across the sky. Go. We'll get there by car."

"I am sure the Alien can handle anything that might await him. The perpetrators might have already fled the scene."

"I'm not sure. Get moving!"

The Alien hovered outside the penthouse lair. There had not

been any forced entry, but someone had entered—from the air, no less.

He had constructed the walls of the lair to withstand the powers of someone such as himself. The walls were lined with lead, retarding any attempts at using his heightened vision spectrum.

The forcefield was down, and the sliding window stood open. He had almost no surveillance advantages. His sensitive hearing was incapable of detecting sounds through the soundproofed walls; he listened at the open window.

Nothing.

For the first time since he'd discovered his superpowers, the Alien felt vulnerable. The situation had all the feeling of a trap. Who could have penetrated the Lair? Were they waiting inside? What for?

He should wait for the others to arrive, but if it was a trap, he feared for them. Better he should spring the trap and render it harmless before they arrived.

He landed inside the penthouse; the window slid shut behind him.

The Lair was a ruined mess. Sparks shot from a chair embedded in the viewscreen. Spiderweb cracks spread out from the point of impact. On the floor and dangling from the ceiling, other lives wires hissed and spat, the lines ripped from equipment. One computer bank had been toppled. Some residual emergency power was still functional: the lights in the ceiling flickered.

Someone with strength had committed the destruction. They might have also been in a rage, but despite the artifice of vandalism there was a logical pattern to the disabling of the equipment. The data center was ruined, but power continued to supply the lights.

The Alien proceeded cautiously.

"No," the Alien muttered.

Whoever had penetrated the forcefield and deciphered the code to the window entry had not had similar fortune gaining access to the power supply. The wall had been smashed open as though a battering ram had been used.

The Alien rushed to the breach and flew into the chamber behind the wall.

The pod was intact. It showed no more damage than it always had—the scorch marks of atmospheric entry and the missing plates where the Alien had repurposed the metal to create the body of the Robot. The main power coupling ran from the pod into the central console of the lair. It had been disconnected but not damaged. The Alien avoided the temptation to reconnect the coupling. His initial rashness fading, he didn't want to touch anything until he had studied the crime scene thoroughly.

He stepped back into the Lair.

An oversized industrial battery unit had not been damaged. Working at heightened speed, the Alien yanked out wires and rigged a temporary audio link.

"This is the Alien. I've rigged an audio transceiver. Can anyone hear me?"

The Protector replied. "Yes. We're on our way. What happened?"

"Vandalism. Systems smashed and...."

The Alien heard an almost imperceptible sound—the quiet whine of an efficient motor. He focused on the sound's origination. The noise halted, but it had come from the direction of the exposed chamber.

The Alien surveyed the hole in the wall, peering inside the room.

The power coupling under the pod had been reconnected. He scanned the room with heightened vision spectrums. His vision could not penetrate the hull of the pod. The metal was unearthly, but not dense. A strange, low-level radiation from the metal blurred his vision and created a sense of vertigo. He had studied the radiation ever since he had discovered it after his arrival on Earth. It had proven harmless, though disconcerting.

The pod was the logical place to hide—it was the only place to hide. Did they know he could not see through the material? No. Who could know?

"Come out of there."

Brakes squealed and tires screeched as the Protector turned hard down a side street. One-way signs indicated the opposite direction.

The Protector's driving skills were top-notch, but at such speed and wild turns the Understudy felt butterflies in her stomach.

"Going the wrong way."

"Radar's clear," the Protector said.

A navigation system with real time traffic hadn't been enough: he'd installed the radar unit, too. The Understudy noticed he hadn't glanced at the map.

"Should we be going this fast?" She tried to keep her voice even. "You're good, but this isn't your city."

"I know the territory well enough."

They ran through two yellow lights. The Understudy winced, expecting to hear cars crashing, but heard nothing. She thought it was a minor miracle there weren't already police on their tail.

"You're really concerned, aren't you?"

The Protector gave a quick nod.

"If someone sets a trap for the Alien, they are either very stupid, or very sure of what they are doing. By now, most of the stupid criminals who believed they could take down the Alien have weeded themselves out."

"That leaves the smart ones."

"I would like to think a smart criminal is an oxymoron, but it isn't always the case."

They raced through two more side streets, then sped onto a main four-lane thoroughfare. The Understudy didn't have time to read street signs. The digital map indicated they were traveling along Frontage Avenue, and their destination was straight ahead.

"Almost there."

The Understudy craned her neck, looking up through the windshield and then the side window, searching the sky. She saw the skyscraper where Pallas Sentinel News Corp was headquartered. At the top, she knew, resided the Alien's penthouse suite—a gift from newspaper editor Cornelius Black, whom the Alien had saved from an attempted murder.

"I don't see the Robot."

A bulb on the dashboard flashed green and the micro-speaker beside it beeped. It was the first time the Understudy had seen the circuit active. The Protector had once told her it was a direct line for emergency communication with an old acquaintance. She wondered, again, what falling out had come between the Alien and the Protector.

"This is the Alien. I've rigged an audio transceiver. Can anyone hear me?"

"Yes." The Protector let out a sigh of relief. "We're on our way. What happened?"

"Vandalism. Systems smashed and…." the Alien paused.

The Protector's eyes flicked to the heads-up display. The Understudy saw the communications unit was functioning. The Alien had not been cut-off.

"What? What's going on?" the Protector asked.

The Alien didn't respond to the query. Instead, he spoke to someone else.

"Come out of there," the Alien commanded to someone.

"Talk to me," the Protector said.

The Alien spoke, his voice tinged with wonder.

"You?"

A strange electronic howl wailed through the speakers. The Understudy jammed her fingertips to her ears. The Protector kept his hands on the steering wheel and winced.

Someone screamed.

The comm unit flashed red. The Alien's link had been severed.

The Robot saw a glimpse of the Alien's green body entering the penthouse lair through the main window. It considered following but opted to utilize the emergency rear entrance. If anyone other than the Alien was in the lair, a pincer approach might catch the perpetrator unaware.

The entry code keypad was offline. The Robot extruded a cable from within its arm and plugged into the port. Phantom power was enough to revive the keypad. Pale light limned the number keys. The Robot entered the code. The door was receiving some power from the Lair, but not enough. It struggled to open, managing a gap of an inch. The Robot slid its fingers through and applied strength. The door mechanisms resisted and groaned in protest, but finally yielded to pressure. The door, more of an emergency hatch, retreated into its slot.

The Robot crept along a short corridor and emerged in the guest quarters. It heard the Alien's voice. Walls muffled the sounds, but the Alien seemed to be in conversation with someone.

A strange light permeated the walls and scintillated along the ceiling. The colors were beyond the ability of human eyes to register. The Robot's artificial nervous system registered something that felt like warmth but was not heat. There was a mechanical whine, already pitched higher than a human could hear and growing shriller.

The Alien screamed.

The Robot ran, its gangly metallic legs stomping the floor with each stride. It burst through the door into the nerve center of the lair. Ignoring the demolished equipment strewn about the room, the Robot rushed to the breached wall and the exposed escape capsule.

An after image of strange energies in the room faded rapidly. The Robot thought it might be an unknown radiation, but it could not analyze the data. There might have been a heat signature leading out the open window, but the trail had been obscured. Instead of trying to follow, the Robot entered the antechamber. It peered into the capsule.

The Alien's uniform had been designed to withstand abuses the Alien often encountered. The Alien was impervious, but it would be embarrassing to have his clothing shot to tatters or burned off in a public spectacle. The material, the Robot assumed, must have been extraterrestrial, or the Alien had manufactured something with Earth resources using advanced techniques humans could not fathom.

One swatch of the Alien's blue shirt, burned at the edges, sat atop a pile of ashes on the floor. The rest of the uniform had been consumed in a conflagration.

And the Alien?

The Robot did not comprehend what it saw. It calculated the mass, scanned burn patterns on the walls, and reached the logical conclusion. If the Robot had been human, it would have rejected that conclusion. Its artificial reasoning did not have the luxury of denying facts.

"The Alien is dead."

6. MEMORIAL

The Protector and the Understudy sprinted across the lobby to a bank of elevators. Ornate wrought brass sconces occupied the space between each set of doors. The elevator door jambs had matching design. The Understudy jabbed every up-arrow button.

"Come on! Come on!" The Understudy grunted in exasperation. Not a single elevator was anywhere near the first floor. "How close can we get?"

"What?" The Protector turned his back to her and fished his hand in his coat pocket.

"These buildings never have the penthouse accessible via public elevator." The Understudy poked out her fingers. "One or two floors away? Then we'll need to breach the stairwell." She stamped her feet and let out a growl of impatience. "Too much time!"

"Yes, too much." The Protector inserted a key into the call panel for the penthouse elevator. The floor indicator light flashed across rapidly as the elevator descended. Within moments, the bell dinged, and the doors slid open.

"How can it be so fast?" the Understudy asked.

The Protector ushered her into the elevator. "I helped with the design. A little."

"That's why you have a key?"

The Understudy pressed the single button on the interior panel. The doors whooshed shut. The elevator shot upward. She wondered if the design included any alien acceleration technology.

"If we're being honest," the Protector said. "The key is more an embezzlement than a payment for services rendered."

"You made a copy of the key," the Understudy said. "Why?"

"Moments like this."

"I'm not sure the Alien would approve."

"I have the feeling he knows."

The doors slid open, and the Protector stepped into the room. The Understudy gasped and hesitated momentarily before stepping out. She had long dreamed of entering the fabled lair of the Alien, never imagining she would find the place in ruins.

A large monitor dominating the room had been smashed; the cracked screen danced in ruined pixilation around an embedded chair. The chair had yielded to gravity and crashed to the floor. Ceiling lights flickered. Equipment had been shoved over, and wires had been pulled out and strewn about the room.

"This is bad." The Protector pulled out an oversized pistol. It was a non-lethal weapon, something akin to a taser but not reliant upon wires. The projectile itself produced the voltage necessary to disable its target. "I should be the only one able to slip in here uninvited."

He skirted spitting, hissing wires. Glass shards crunched under his soles. The Understudy followed. They picked their way around keyboards, wireless units, and other electronic debris strewn about the room.

"Someone threw a temper tantrum," the Understudy said. "Maybe they didn't find what they were looking for."

"Or maybe this is what they wanted—vandalism and ruining the Alien's lair."

The Understudy caught movement in her peripheral vision, spun with a telescoping stanchion ready in hand. A hole had been torn in the wall, large enough to walk through. The jagged passageway framed the Robot. It turned its head, seeming to study each of them in turn with its single red eye.

"Where is he?" the Protector asked.

"You are too late," the Robot said. "I was too late."

The Robot turned away. They followed through the breach in the wall. In a once-hidden antechamber, a round metallic capsule perched on a base. There were scorch marks on the outer surface, and the cone-shaped protrusions of a rocket engine on one end of the capsule.

"Is that...?" the Understudy said. "He came here in that, didn't he? To Earth, I mean."

The Protector nodded.

"And he died there," the Robot said.

The Protector and the Understudy exchanged glances. Stomach churning, the Understudy stepped forward with the Protector. They peered inside.

The interior of the capsule was simple: a reclined seat and an uncomplicated set of controls, large buttons with alien symbols. The material of the seat was warped as though partially melted. A pile of grey and white ash shifted from the seat, and a singed swatch of blue material slipped to the floor.

The implication hit the Understudy in the gut. She reeled back and fought nausea. She needed to choke down something that wanted to come up. She pulled her head out of the capsule and whirled around.

"How?" she asked the Robot.

"I arrived too late," the Robot repeated. It held out its hands as though it could not find the correct words to speak—like a person in shock.

"Did you see anything at all?" The Protector's voice was muffled in the alien pod.

"Odd lights and sounds. I heard the Alien speaking—as if to someone."

The Understudy looked around the room, her panic rising. If someone could kill—outright destroy—the Alien, what chance would two humans stand?

"It is all right," the Robot assured her. "There is no one here now. They must have slipped away, back out the window, while I examined the pod."

"And while we were on our way up," the Protector said.

"Who else can fly?" the Understudy asked. "We didn't see a helicopter waiting to extract someone."

The Protector shrugged. "No one we know of—yet."

"It must be a mistake!" The Understudy fought down her panic. She hadn't known the Alien personally, but the world felt vulnerable and unsafe without his presence. She felt a warm tear running down her cheek. "It's a trick."

The Robot eyed her impassively, though its head seemed bowed in mourning. It was perhaps scanning the interior of the capsule, again, searching for something—anything it might have missed. Or perhaps not. The Robot was a machine, after all.

The Protector shook his head slowly. He glanced around the interior of the pod one more time and then turned to face the Understudy and the Robot.

"No deception. He's gone." The Protector's expression was stern and grim. "The Alien is dead."

The Understudy thought the weather considerate. It was gray, overcast, and chilly, but the rain held off for the morning. The overnight wind had helped strip bare the autumn trees in the park. The wind had subsided into a breeze, skittering leaves along the streets of the procession. The somber morning matched the mood of the city.

Encased in an urn bearing the symbol that had once emblazoned his chest, the Alien's remains were solemnly marched through the streets and placed at a site in the heart of Pallas's Rose Park. When evening came the urn would be returned to the Robot for safekeeping. Later, a granite monument would be built on the site to house the urn—funding provided by the ever-altruistic Milton Medina.

The Understudy wondered if the Protector was biting his tongue as hard as she was biting hers. And what did the Robot think? She wondered what the Robot felt, but remembered the machine lacked emotion—supposedly.

A procession of thousands packed the streets to walk, to observe, and to mourn. The Robot carried the urn. The Robot's public appearance was a story unto itself, as it had never emerged from the penthouse lair of the Alien, as far as the public knew.

The duo from Crowsport mingled through the crowd, appearing in public as a show of support. The Protector also wanted a heightened presence. Lunatics might consider pulling a deadly stunt in the throng.

The Understudy didn't like seeing the Robot walking alone. It was strange that, among a populace grateful for the Alien's sacrifice, she wasn't sure if the Alien could have considered any of them a friend. The Alien's closest friend seemed to have been the Protector, yet even their friendship had cooled to a professional acquaintance. The Protector kept his regret buried. The public might not see it, but the Understudy knew it was there.

They listened to the police commissioner and various city politicians make their speeches. Knowing what she knew, the Understudy was glad Medina didn't have a speaking role in the ceremonies. His lying face would have sent her over the edge.

They took a break, resting on a park bench on the edge of the crowd.

"What about Medina?" the Understudy asked quietly.

"What about him?"

"If that centaur-bot had security footage, Medina might know the Alien wasn't the only one breaching his factory the other night."

"He probably does know," the Protector admitted. "We should be on guard, but he knows we don't have anything on him. Trying to get at us or the Robot would increase his chance of being discovered. I think he'll stay under the radar."

The rain started. The crowd dispersed. Many went away with shoulders hunched against the weather, giving their postures an aura of defeat.

At the memorial, only two others remained at the Robot's side—Lester, the mustached police commissioner, and Jackman, the cigar-chomping editor of the Pallas Globe newspaper. The two men saw the Protector and the Understudy approach. They gave curt nods of acknowledgement and bade the Robot farewell. They didn't stop for conversation as they walked past the duo from Crowsport.

"Not fans of ours," the Understudy commented, turning her head to watch the men walk away.

"No." The Protector chuckled. "The Alien was a deputized vigilante, a valued citizen of the shining city of Pallas. You and I are just a couple of Crowsport vigilantes."

She glanced ahead. The Robot stood at the makeshift monument which overflowed with tributes of flowers and personal notes. The ink on the sentiments bled under the increasing rainfall.

"I think the Robot feels the loss."

"It shouldn't have emotions, but who knows what tricks the Alien put inside that shell. It must at least feel a difference with disruption of its routine."

"You're really going to leave him here alone?"

"We need to look after Crowsport." The Protector shrugged. "Not every city gets a superhero, kid. Pallas had its day with the Alien. It will need to look after itself now."

The Robot turned at their approach, seeming to break his concentration as a ruminating person might. The red light of his single eye and the red lines along his black body stood out in the gathering gloom of late afternoon.

"I'm sorry," the Understudy said. "And I'm sorry I don't know what else to say."

"Words are not necessary, but thank you," the Robot said. The sentiment felt awkward and unnecessary. The machine—with its limited expression and lack of emotion—could not convey any warmth in its statement. "You will be returning to Crowsport?"

"Yes," the Understudy said. She felt sad. She wanted to feel sad for the Robot, too, because it could not feel.

"I'm sorry we can't bring M..." the Protector closed his mouth. They were in a public place, after all, even if the crowd had dwindled. "I'm sorry we can't stay to help bring the Alien's killers to justice. There aren't any loose ends to grab—for now."

"It is a police matter now," the Robot said, "Though I doubt they will find any leads, as you have said."

"What will you do?" the Understudy asked.

She was convinced the Robot would have sighed if it had the capacity. As it was, she could swear the machine gave a slight shrug.

"Unknown. For now, I will retire to the Lair and perform repairs. I will continue to probe for evidence. Maybe I will uncover something to give to the police."

"I think the network and computer trails will be cold and locked down now," the Protector said. "The police will want proper warrants."

"Of course."

"You should try some field work." The Protector nodded toward the memorial. "He would have wanted that."

"Our first field foray did not end well." The Robot slowly shook its black head. "Besides, the Alien had planned for a partnership and mentoring. It cannot come to fruition now."

The Protector waved his hand.

"Just get out there. You might surprise yourself."

"Where would I start?"

"Where the Alien left off," the Understudy said. The Protector nodded in agreement.

"I am not deputized by the city police," the Robot said.

"Neither was he, when he started," the Protector said.

"I will consider that course of action." The Robot turned its red eye on the Protector. "Do you have any parting advice?"

The Protector tucked his chin against the rain, thinking of a response. Then he nodded.

"You've heard of 'good cop, bad cop'?"

"Yes," said the Robot.

"When you work alone," the Protector said. "Being the bad cop is best course of action."

In the Lair, the Robot repaired what equipment it could. It had been one thing to sit, supporting the Alien and awaiting his return from missions. Staying in the penthouse with no actions to perform did not seem correct. The Protector's advice seemed to have triggered a programmatic process. Something drove the Robot to take action.

The Robot sometimes wondered how much of its programming had been designed to evolve beyond algorithms. Could there have been some failsafe, some subconscious program invoked when the Alien died?

The Robot refocused its attention. Analysis and theorizing could come later. The databases were back online, but it had eidetic memory. It did not require the systems of the Lair to analyze what it already knew. There had a been a link between Dufresne and Medina—the accountant, Stumper. The link might be also be a lead toward proving who had murdered the Alien.

It was time for field work.

The Robot flew off the roof of the skyscraper.

"Finally," muttered the Protector.

He'd waited in a dark alley, observing the lofty penthouse. It appeared the Robot had taken his advice. What else would it be doing at this hour? He'd figure that out soon enough.

This time, the Protector did not rush through the front doors, but covertly came in through a rear entrance. He slipped to the penthouse elevator unseen and rode up to the Lair.

The mess had been cleaned. The smashed equipment had been removed, leaving gaps where there had been spaces choked with monitors and computers. Sheets of plywood covered the space where the panoramic window had been. Wind whistled through small gaps in the arrangement. The temperature was cool, but that wouldn't bother the Robot.

The Protector accessed what data he could. After a few minutes, he thumped a fist on the tabletop where he was working.

"I know all this," he said. "Come on, Alien. Where's the good stuff? Where's the stuff you didn't want anyone to find?"

The Protector ran his fingers along the brim of his fedora.

"No, not out here."

He walked over to the smashed interior wall. It had not been covered with plywood. He stepped through and stared at the alien escape pod.

"This is where your secrets are, isn't it?" The Protector sighed. He looked upward. "Probably in some alien computer in an alien language, right?"

Though the room had not been cleaned yet, the Protector was relieved to see the bits of cloth and ash of the Alien's remains had been removed from the interior of the pod.

He climbed inside the capsule and shifted into the seat. The pod still had power—the Lair ran on it. Presumably, the pod wasn't configured to fly again. At least, the Protector convinced himself of that before he tried buttons at random.

A small display screen came to life. It seemed to be something like a heads-up display on a military fighter jet, with combined pictograms and data in alien characters. The visuals looped.

"A flight log."

The Protector didn't see how it could be anything else. Escape pods were designed to escape. What else would they have to record?

He watched the loop until he memorized the sequence. If he ran it through his mind's eye enough times, maybe it would make sense.

The wall hiding the pod had been smashed. The Alien had been caught in a trap. But was there more? Had the Alien's murderer been viewing this same data? Had there been more purpose to the intruder's trespass than killing the Alien?

The Protector climbed out of pod. He stood with his hands on his hips, surveying the room.

"The brains were out there, but the heart was in here. It's a large piece of nostalgia to keep around, even if it is a good power source."

The Protector circled around the pod.

"You hid it behind a wall. But you would have wanted to keep an eye on it."

He looked up at the ceiling corners. In the back, to the right, a smashed camera still hung from wires.

"Far too obvious, my friend." The Protector chuckled. "But perhaps your murderer didn't know how you think."

The Protector pressed his palms against the rear wall, waving his arms, trying to touch every inch as he walked along.

At the corner, his hand bumped something solid—something that protruded slightly. Something that was not there when he looked at it.

"Camouflage."

He looked down at the black and white tiled floor. There was an incongruous half-tile of black against the wall. Within moments he found a hidden catch and lifted out the tile. In the cubby hole underneath, wires ran down from the wall into a small disk drive.

The Protector smiled and disconnected the drive. In moments, he was back in the main room of the Lair, hooking the device into the system.

"Time to see what you saw—if anything."

The video ran through a fisheye lens. There was no sound recording. The camera had activated as the wall was breached. Flying debris must have triggered the motion detector. Frustratingly, the blind spot of the camera overlapped with the intrusion. A shape flitted past. A few minutes later, the Alien stepped into the room. He hesitated. His mouth moved. He tensed and stepped forward, too close to the pod to be seen any longer.

The video scrambled. The rest of the scene unintelligible. The Protector assumed whatever energy had killed the Alien had also overloaded the camera. Fortunately, the disk had survived.

He played the entrance of the furtive shape again. It was fast, only partially seen, and not clear in the semi-dark. But he thought there was something familiar.

The Protector let a long breath whistle past his teeth. He didn't see how it was possible—but it was a possibility.

"Perhaps I've overstayed my welcome," he said. "One more stop before my coffee break."

The Frontier Building, Pallas's premiere and most exclusive apartment building, was a holdover from an earlier age, marked by high gables and dormers. It had been built in a sparsely populated area of the city and nicknamed "The Frontier." Decades of urban growth had stolen away its isolation, and though it was still tall, taller structures surrounded it. The Frontier had a gothic flare no other edifice in Pallas could match.

The Robot considered that Stumper must mean more to Medina than the Alien had realized. The Frontier was not a place one would expect to find a lower-tier gangster accountant on the run.

Under cover of darkness, the Robot landed on a balustraded balcony.

The security system, modern technology grafted onto an

outdated framework, was not difficult to penetrate. The Robot initiated the shutdown, turning off the alarm on the slider door. The Robot reached long mechanical fingers toward the glass. Its hand hovered before the window.

Stumper was an excellent computer tech. Online receipts had shown purchases of various electronic components that could be used to create security systems off the grid. Stumper would want to stay isolated. He would not want any trace of his existence to leak back to Dufresne.

The Robot opened a secure link back to the Lair and re-examined the downloaded receipts. A sound dish would be the most likely construct utilized with the known materials Stumper had purchased recently.

The Robot gazed through the glass of the doors and wondered if it had approached quietly enough. A gap between the drapes revealed something round on the kitchen counter facing the window. Possibly the sound dish. Perhaps not.

Any scan beyond a visual might trigger an alarm.

The Robot faced a dilemma—continue to use stealth or make a bold move?

The sliding door lacked any electronics or security alarm. The lock was on the inside. There might be a security bar wedged in the running groove. For someone involved with industrial technology, Stumper knew when simple and old-fashioned were the better option. The Robot's strength could tear open the door and snap the bar, but all surprise would be lost.

It reached for the door.

A voice squawked through a thin line speaker installed along the top of the door.

"No-no." The speaker had a whiny timbre. "Touch that handle and you'll get fried. I'm not sure how you are constructed, but I believe a strong jolt will scramble at least some of your circuits."

The Robot pulled its hand back. Red laser beams stabbed out from tiny portholes around the jamb, forming a box that enclosed the balcony.

"No leaving, either. Each baluster is a fragmentation bomb.

Trip the laser and the explosion will be instantaneous. You won't escape the shockwave. It might not kill you, but you wouldn't want all that shrapnel landing on pedestrians below. And you certainly wouldn't want to be one of those pieces of shrapnel. With your heavy metal body, you're bound to squash someone like a bug."

Stumper exaggerated. The chances of the Robot crashing on a passing pedestrian were low, but Stumper knew there was a chance, however small. The Robot could not put anyone at unnecessary risk.

"I came here to talk with you," the Robot said. "Violence is not necessary."

"I'll be the judge of that," Stumper replied. "I can hear you. You can hear me. Talk."

"I don't wish to broadcast your business to the outside world, Mr. Fulcrum."

"What business is that?"

"Your name change, for a start, Mr. Stumper."

The lasers turned off. A crackling sound and whiff of ozone came from the door handle. A shape moved behind the drapes and knelt. There had been a security bar. The lock on the handle clicked. The shape moved away from the door.

"Come in. It's safe," Stumper said. He sounded wary but not defeated. "For now."

The Robot entered the room into a formal dining room with a heavy oak table. Stumper sat at one end. As revealed in his personnel photo, the former clean-cut look had given way to the assumed identity of Fulcrum. Contact lenses or surgically corrected vision replaced his eyeglasses, and he wore a thick beard and long hair.

"So, you're the Alien's robot?" Stumper asked. He appraised the Robot with a studious gaze, doubtless trying to guess at some of the technology hidden inside the black-and-red-highlighted machine before him. "Saw you on the news."

"It is the Alien's death that brings me here."

"What does that have to do with me?"

"I have reason to believe Milton Medina had some part in the assassination."

Stumper pondered, pursed his lips.

"Medina is working with Dufresne now—your former employer," the Robot said.

"Yes." Stumper rolled his eyes in exaggerated annoyance. "When you said my real name, it was obvious you must know about my past."

"Medina is making surface-to-air missiles and smuggling them through Dufresne's control of the railroad."

"That's a bit old fashioned."

"Ever since air travel security tightened, even private planes undergo scrutiny. He cannot air-freight his contraband. The railroad to Crowsport gives him access to all manner of cargo ships heading to foreign ports."

"And greased port-authority hands," Stumper commented blithely. His grin faltered slightly. His cockiness had momentarily betrayed him.

"You know about that?" the Robot asked.

"Only from the old days." Stumper faked an insouciant shrug. "I wouldn't know anything about that now."

Stumper crossed his arms and smiled. The Robot did not consider itself a well-versed judge of human behavior, but it seemed Stumper would say nothing more.

What would the Alien have done at reaching such an impasse?

The Robot considered the data.

"Arms smuggling is not easy work. It would be easier to run drugs. A rocket launcher cannot be hidden in a pocket. You have a history with Dufresne. Medina could use leverage to coerce someone into helping his operation. Like a known criminal with a penchant for staying out of prison. If Medina had influence over a person like that, he would have a smuggling operation at his fingertips."

"All conjecture. You are neither the police nor a lawyer. You weren't invited here, either." Stumper pointed to the balcony. "You can leave the way you came. Now. Before I involve the police."

"I do not think Medina would want you anywhere near the police."

"Maybe, but I've said all I'm going to say to you. This chat has already taken too long."

Once again, Stumper's expression exuded stubbornness and confidence. There did not appear to be any logical path to continue the conversational interrogation. The Robot again extrapolated an imaginary situation, substituting the Alien in its place.

"It cannot be easy for you," the Robot said.

"What are you talking about?"

"Hiding from one powerful man and living under the foot of another."

Stumper laughed. "Look around you. I'm in the Frontier, all expenses paid. The life of the Pallas elite. Do you think being Medina's flunky bothers me? I'm living life larger than large."

"Then you should enjoy it while it lasts. It could all be over tomorrow at Medina's whim. I surmise that a layoff from Medina's employment would be fatal for you. You are not someone who can be simply let go."

"Medina would have no reason to do that!"

"I was able to track you down," the Robot said. "Now you are a potential loose end. It wouldn't take much of a tip-off to let Dufresne know you'd faked your death. With the information concerning Dufresne's operations at Medina's disposal, it is surprising Dufresne has not already come to that realization."

Conflicting emotions passed over Stumper's face. His grin disappeared into an angry frown.

"You set me up!"

"What do you know?" the Robot demanded.

Stumper considered for a moment.

"Come with me."

Stumper led the Robot through the spacious apartment, down a hallway, and into the room at the end.

The Robot spotted various security detection devices all around the apartment. Some cameras were real. Some were dummies. Some were real, disguised as dummies. There were plenty of microphones, too.

"Are you recording my visit?"

"Visit? Quaint." Stumper opened the door at the end of the hall. "Of course I am. Aren't you? Probably on a disk in your chest or in your head with a backup stream being sent out to the famous penthouse lair of the Alien."

The Robot stepped into the room after Stumper. The room served as an office. A file cabinet stood in one corner. Various computer chassis of various makes and eras were spread haphazardly around the room. A small desk featured a powerful new streamlined model with a large monitor.

It was not unlike the setup at the Lair.

The Robot lacked instinct. Yet, somehow, a warning emerged through its mechanical being. How proficient at tech hacking was Stumper? As talented as the Alien? As capable as the Robot? Better? The Robot favored wariness, constantly analyzing and re-analyzing the data and situation in which it found itself.

Stumper's hand thrust up spraying a black, viscous fluid from a miniature spray can. The gummy syrup dripped down over the Robot's single red eye.

"Visual impairment," the Robot reported. "You should know I have plenty of other instruments to image my surroundings."

The Robot struck his fist against Stumper's solar plexus. The man somersaulted back into the hall. The Robot grabbed a free-standing lamp and pulled the cord from the wall. It leaned over Stumper, bent the lamp pole around his torso, and pinned his arms.

The Robot lifted Stumper to his feet and marched him into the office. There were two chairs. The Robot deposited Stumper in one.

Stumper groaned, shook his head.

"You're lucky I didn't break my face on the way to the floor," said Stumper. "Breaking and entering, and now assault and battery. You're in a lot of trouble."

"I was invited in." The Robot typed at the computer. "You fell down."

"I fell down?" Stumper guffawed. "Did the Alien teach you that?"

"No," the Robot said. "The Protector did."

Stumper did not reply. He watched the Robot's attempts to access the computer.

"You'll be here all night." Stumper's confidence was a taunt. "You'll be here until I am missed at work. Then Medina will send someone to check on me."

The Robot ignored Stumper. Black fingers danced over the keyboard, trying various techniques to bypass encrypted access codes and protected files. Some data was easily gleaned, but anything incriminating had been buried deep. Holes in the defenses were plugged as soon as the Robot created them.

The Robot could not breach the firewall completely, but the bits and pieces it could reveal behaved similarly to Medina's systems. Stumper had contributed largely to Medina's security.

"Good to know," the Robot commented.

"Good to know what?" asked Stumper.

The Robot let him wonder. It tried various solutions until one finally broke through. Icons representing files disappeared from the desktop display on the monitor.

Stumper's confident grin fell. "What have you done?"

"I removed all traces of my visit here and disabled any further recordings until I leave. They will be enabled when you restart the security systems."

Stumper glanced at the screen and gave a reluctant nod of respect.

"You're as good a hacker as I am."

"But those are the only files of consequence on this computer." The Robot pointed at the screen. "The remaining files are all red herrings."

"Of course, I wouldn't keep anything sensitive on a computer accessible from wireless or wired connection." Stumper laughed. "Laptop. It's completely isolated."

"Where?"

"Why should I tell you?"

The Robot surveyed the room. There was no laptop left out in the open. No closet in the room. It pinged an echolocation and found no hidden room. Aside from the desk and tables for the sprawling equipment, the only other furniture was a metal file cabinet.

The Robot pulled on the bottom drawer, tearing off the face with a screeching twist of metal.

"Hey!"

In the drawer was a laptop computer. It had no brand logo; it had been home-assembled. An incongruous plastic flower of multi-colored petals protruded from the lid where a corporate logo would have been, giving brightness to the black metallic housing.

"No Wi-Fi, no cables. Thumb drive in and out if something needs transferring," Stumper said. "Old-fashioned and secure."

"As long as you do not lose the thumb drive."

"Of course," Stumper smiled. "How about you untie me? I'd rather you not smash your way into my laptop, too."

"You will cooperate?" the Robot asked.

"For now. I don't think I can go anywhere." Stumper gave a nervous laugh. "To be honest, what you said has got me thinking. I'm wondering just how valuable or disposable I am to Medina."

The Robot nodded and freed Stumper. The tech wizard sat at the desk, pressed the power button on the laptop. The Robot stood on the other side of the desk, waiting.

The Robot heard the whine of the laptop powering up, but Stumper was typing before the computer was ready for input.

The Robot reached across the table, trying to knock the laptop away, but only succeeded in spinning it around, the back facing Stumper. A stream of water sprayed from the center of the plastic flower. The water doused Stumper's face as a blinding electric bolt discharged from the computer's metallic frame and conducted along the water. There was a stench of ozone and burned flesh. Steam lingered in the air. Stumper had no time to cry out. His body spasmed out of the chair and onto the floor until the electric current and water stopped flowing.

The Robot scanned Stumper's smoking body. There were no vital signs.

An alarm sounded, something crashed in the kitchen. Muttered curses and footsteps approached. The Robot glanced up.

The Protector stood at the threshold to the office, the

doorway framing his fedora-and-trench-coat silhouette. He surveyed the scene and pursed his lips.

"You know," the Protector said. "This looks more than a bit suspicious from where I'm standing."

7. DEDUCTIONS AND DISAGREEMENTS

From the doorway, the Protector stared at the Robot. He looked past the Robot's shoulder, nodded at the electrocuted corpse of Alan Stumper.

"Care to explain yourself?"

"I came here to interrogate Stumper. He works—worked—for Medina, but he used—"

The Protector cut off the sentence with a hand wave. "I'm aware who he used to work for. And who he works for now. Why'd you kill him?"

"I did not kill him." The Robot turned its palm upward and extended its fingers, indicating the laptop. "Not intentionally. I defended myself."

The Protector fell into a stony silence. He stepped into the office.

"Be careful," the Robot warned. "There might be more traps."

The Robot had not thought to scan for more traps. Between interrogating Stumper, Stumper's death, and the Protector's arrival, the Robot had not had time for a search.

The Protector stepped more cautiously. He examined the body, then he studied the boobytrapped laptop in its melted and warped plastic casing. He searched the room, exposed other dangerous traps. Some used guns, others were connected to explosives, and there were more electrocution setups. The Protector deactivated the lethal tricks.

"This guy was a piece of work."

"Why are you here?"

"I found the data about Stumper in the Lair. I figured this is where you were headed."

"Why were you in the Lair?" the Robot asked. "You said you were returning to Crowsport."

"I lied." The Protector nudged the brim of his fedora up a half inch. "Get used to it if you're going to do field work. People fib."

"Did you stay to investigate Stumper, too?"

The Protector crossed his arms.

"No, I stayed to investigate you."

The Robot tipped its head quizzically. "Why?"

"You were there when the Alien died. Frankly, I consider you a suspect."

The Robot cocked its head slightly. "No, I was not there. I arrived too late."

"That's what you said."

"I am not programmed to lie."

"That's what your programming tells you—what the Alien told you. But what if you didn't even know?"

"How would I not know?"

"At first I wondered if Medina had gotten to you. Slipped a programming bug inside your metal head one of those times you tried to breach his network. Maybe he did. Or, maybe you've been this way from the start."

"Why would I kill my creator?"

"Good question. I don't know. Maybe you didn't kill him. Not you standing before me—another you."

The Robot shook its head. "I do not follow this train of thought."

"Think of it as robot Jekyll and Hyde. Maybe you don't even know. Maybe you shut down while another program takes over."

"There would be data."

"Not if it was erased before you resumed control."

"If I worked for Medina, why would I murder this man?"

"Loose end. Maybe Medina figured out the Alien could have traced Stumper, then so could someone else," the Protector said.

"I did not kill this man. It was an accident."

"Okay. We'll take Stumper out of the picture—for now," the Protector said. "Let's get back to the Alien."

"Go on."

"We don't even know what could have killed the Alien. That's some specialized knowledge. I know. I've researched it in case he ever went rogue. I never found an answer."

"Maybe Medina did."

The Protector laughed. "I suppose it's possible—but only because he had more time and money. Not because he could outthink me."

The Protector pointed a gloved finger at the Robot. "Or maybe the Alien had a file on its own weaknesses—a file you had access to."

"You have no proof."

The Protector's shoulders slumped. "No. And I can't even say I have a hunch. I'm operating like you on this one—logic."

"Your logic is...flimsy."

"It's what I have to work with," the Protector said. "It's not only the Alien's murder. I investigated that laser theft. Someone got through Medina's security, into the facility, and left with an industrial laser. Not a sliver of a trace, physical or digital. There are few people who could do that, even from the inside."

"What is the correlation to the Alien's murder? A laser would do him no more harm than anything else could."

"I don't know. It had the Alien concerned, though, or he wouldn't have mentioned it."

"So, you believe the theft is connected."

The Protector nodded. "He also mentioned the observatory break-in. Another clean job—except for the log erasing. That was an oversight. The perpetrator should have faked log entries, not erased them. Even so, operating the telescope and clearing the log took a technical knowledge level surpassing your run-of-the-mill criminal."

"There is still no correlation between these crimes."

"The Alien thought there was."

"He did not mention that to me."

"Nor to me. I could sense it in his tone, his body language.

He was on the cusp of putting them together but hadn't quite aligned the puzzle pieces correctly."

The Robot had not yet fully learned to interpret body language. The Protector could have been correct.

"You believe he had a hunch."

"Yes."

"Do you have a hunch?"

The Protector shook his head. "I wouldn't be here questioning you if I did."

He gingerly stepped toward the door of the office.

"Do me a favor. Make another sweep for booby traps before the cops get here. We don't need anyone else getting killed."

"I will. Where are you going?"

"I'll be heading back to Crowsport now—for real this time," the Protector said.

"And leave me loose—if I am a criminal?"

"It's not like I can hold you. Think about what I've told you. Find a way to figure it out. If you're an honest robot, you'll turn yourself in to the authorities if you find the evidence."

The Robot looked at Stumper's body. It had killed. Self-defense, yes. But its mission was to protect humanity. It could not have known deflecting Stumper's attack would be fatal. Was that true? It had the sensors, the cybernetic brain, the ability to process data faster than any human. Had it, perhaps, known what was coming and allowed it?

There were conflicting points of data, odd areas where programming felt inadequate. Yet, in those places the Robot almost felt something emerging. On the edge of some new paradigm, something beyond logical extrapolation. Emotion and imagination as inputs? But how?

How did not matter. What mattered was an available option besides what the Protector had suspected.

"What if I find evidence to the contrary? Or definitive evidence which offers a different logical explanation?"

The Protector said nothing.

The Robot looked to the doorway.

The Protector had slipped away.

The Understudy wanted to go home. She felt wrung out. The thrill of traveling to Pallas, meeting the Alien and fighting alongside him, had disappeared with the Alien's death and memorial service. It was too close and too real. She wondered what she was doing, fighting against people who observed no laws, who would kill her while she was trying her best to subdue—but not kill—them. If the invulnerable Alien could be murdered, what chance did she have?

The Protector fought crime, but maybe he was living on borrowed time. The thought chilled her. The realities of danger and death were eclipsing the excitement and fun, the thrill of their vigilante actions. She didn't want to attend his funeral. She felt a ghost slide over her grave. Her parents had no idea of her alter ego. They would expect her to fly home for winter holidays, as usual. Turkey gravy and French toast breakfast were her specialties. What would they do if she was gone?

Was it time to quit while she was ahead?

A string of bells over the coffeehouse door announced a new arrival. Some people glanced up from their steaming cups. Most though, kept conversing or typing on their laptops and other devices.

The Protector strode over to the counter, ordered a danish and a black cup of coffee. Incognito, he drew no attention. He'd replaced his fedora with a scally cap, and a tweed jacket stood in for his trench coat. The Understudy had stowed away her goggles and aviator cap and replaced her leather pants with jeans, but she still wore her leather jacket.

The Protector surveyed the room and gave a quick approving nod. She'd chosen a table in the back corner. The crowd had dwindled since she had first arrived. They could talk in relative private if they weren't too loud.

"What was so special you had to go alone?" the Understudy asked as the Protector bit into his danish.

"Had to talk to the Robot," the Protector muttered around his food. He took a swallow of coffee. The heat of the liquid didn't seem to bother his mouth or throat. If it was punching a hole in his stomach, he gave no sign.

"Without me. About what?"

"I think the Robot might be dangerous."

"What?" She had almost blurted out the word in surprise, but she managed to keep her voice low.

"There have been certain incidents. I'm not sure we've gotten the whole story."

"Incidents? You mean crimes."

"Crimes that required a level of sophistication, knowledge, and ability to pull off. Not just pull off. To pull off and hardly leave a ripple in the criminal's wake."

"Why the Robot?"

"Because the crimes all have ties to the Alien, and the Robot is one big tie to the Alien."

The Understudy shook her head.

"Explain it to me."

The Protector did. He dissected the crimes and laid out his theories: the missing laser, the observatory break-in, the assassination of the Alien. Those all could have been Medina, or someone unknown. But he'd found the Robot hovering over the remains of the Alien, and over a dead man, too.

"Circumstantial evidence." The Understudy ate her last bite of blueberry muffin. Her iced coffee had too much of a burnt taste, but she wanted the caffeine and hadn't felt like complaining. "You think the Robot is the only one who could commit the crimes and you're assuming he did. Just because he can does not mean he did. You don't know."

"No, I don't," the Protector admitted. "But the Robot is as much a suspect as anyone else right now. By design, I can't read the Robot. I can't feel a hunch either way."

"And that's disconcerting to you."

"It sure is."

The Understudy wriggled her nose. "So, what are we going to do?"

"Go back to Crowsport," the Protector said.

"What about the Alien's murder? What about the Robot? We're just supposed to leave?"

"It's not our business. We've overstayed our welcome as it is. Pallas needs to stand up and take care of itself now that the Alien is gone. They did before. They can again."

"The Alien changed this city—a lot."

"He did. For the better. Maybe the change will hold. Maybe it won't. People are fickle, but they need to be their own catalyst for change. They can't wait around for a savior."

"Aren't we playing savior in Crowsport?"

"Not at all. I'm not a beacon and I'm not campaigning for change. That's up to the populace. I'm only a fighter in the trenches."

"I thought the Alien was your friend—even if you had differences."

"We had colossal differences." The Protector chuckled and smiled wistfully. "I will avenge him—if the Pallas police don't figure it out. They probably won't. But we can't spend weeks here while Crowsport slides into the hands of organized gangsters and street criminals. We can get back to the Alien's murder later."

"The trail will be cold then."

"I've picked up cold trails before. Don't worry. I'm good at it."

The Understudy scowled and folded her arms. Ten minutes earlier she wanted to go home; now the idea of leaving the fight unfinished gnawed at her. She liked the Robot. Everything the Protector had said was plausible, but she could not bring herself to believe his theory. She felt obliged to prove her mentor wrong.

"Look," the Protector's fingers tapped the table lightly. "We know Medina was part of it. He might not have pulled the trigger, but it was no coincidence we had that brouhaha at the factory at the same time the Alien's lair was trashed. Medina is still the link. Right now, though, we've got nothing on him and he's on high alert. If we give it some time, he might relax a little and slip."

The Understudy regarded him.

"We'll circle back. I promise," the Protector said. "I owe the Alien." He flashed her a wide grin. "So, what do you say, kid. Are you ready to go home?"

The Understudy took a long time before she gave her answer.

Wordlessly, Josephine slid the tablet across the desk to Medina.

He read the reports, scrolled through the information. He set the tablet down and let out a breath through his nostrils. He might have been calming himself, or his anger might have been welling up and he needed to snort it out like a bull preparing to charge.

"Stumper was more paranoid than I imagined," Medina said.

Josephine's face was lined with distaste. She disliked sloppiness and had never approved of declaring any madness to have a method. Stumper had been a genius on the edge of mental illness. It was a wonder the lethal dangers spread throughout his apartment hadn't killed him long before.

"His apartment was littered with traps," she said.

"And he was careless enough to catch himself in one."

"Not entirely."

Josephine took a photograph from the attaché case she was carrying. She handed it to Medina.

"All the traps were deactivated before the police arrived. Stumper wouldn't have done that. Someone had been there—someone with an interest in public safety."

She paused. Medina waved a finger to indicate she continue.

"The electrocuting laptop was fried, of course. Using our contacts in the police evidence impound, I had few moments alone with the computer."

"Did you get it working?"

"No, not a chance. But that wasn't what I was looking for." Josephine smiled. She was proud of her clandestine detective work. "Stumper liked redundancy. There was a micro-computer hidden inside the laptop casing. A bare-essential little unit, but it did have a concealed camera."

Medina studied the gray scale photograph. The subject was blurred.

"If I squint, it almost looks like…."

"It is." Josephine retrieved another photograph from her case. "I've had the photo enhanced."

She handed him the second photograph. Medina only needed a momentary glance.

"Well." Medina dropped both photographs on the desk and

spun his chair to look out the window. "The Alien's robot."

"The Robot was in Stumper's apartment," she said. "The last photo the micro-computer took—the last thing Stumper probably saw—was the Robot."

"Do you think the Robot is a killer?" Medina shook his head. "I don't believe the Alien would have allowed that."

"I can't say. The Alien no longer controls the Robot." Josephine shrugged, scratched her red hair. "I think the Robot caught Stumper in his own trap by accident."

"That is the more likely scenario."

"The real question is—was the Robot scared off, or did they have time to talk?"

"Talk? You mean, did the Robot ask questions?" Medina said. "About me?"

"Yes."

Medina crossed his arms. His tie bunched under his chin. He curled his wrist, pulled the tie taut with a free hand. Then he spun his chair to face Josephine again.

"I think it is safe to assume the Robot is following in its mentor's footsteps."

"It appears so."

"Those attempts at hacking into our networks. I thought the Alien had done that—until I saw the Robot. The Robot probably did the dirty work."

"It could represent a security risk."

"But it's a machine. It lives on data and logic. It wouldn't have the intuition. It couldn't have figured out much on its own." Medina scowled. "The Protector. As if he doesn't have enough to do in Crowsport."

"The Robot might have been following information the Alien left behind."

Medina uncrossed his arms, drummed his fingers on the desktop, one eyebrow cocked in thought. Josephine waited, standing at attention—a soldier awaiting orders.

"I want this problem eliminated," he said at last.

"Of course."

"I want you to handle it personally, Josephine." Medina slapped his palm on the desk. "I'm not subcontracting this job to gangster buffoons—or anyone else."

"We don't know what the Robot can do, but we must assume it won't be easy to dispatch," Josephine said. "Do you have something in mind?"

"I most certainly do." Medina's mouth cocked in a half-smile. The crooked grin contained more malice than mirth. "I have a new product that needs field testing. This will be a perfect opportunity."

The Protector was back home. It didn't exactly feel right, but it felt correct and necessary. He stood still for a while, absorbing the ambience of Crowsport at night. Lights and shadows, sirens in the distance, growls of automobiles. Voices in the night coming and going on the wind around street corners. Scents and odors, too. Where he stood, the overwhelming stench was of diesel fuel.

He found a section of chain link fence where vagrants had clipped out enough wire to allow a person to shimmy under. The damage would be repaired in due time, but this latest vandalism had yet to be discovered. He crawled under, rose up on the other side, and brushed dirt from the front of his coat.

He still thought about the Robot, and what he'd told the Understudy, and her reaction. He didn't like distrusting the Robot, but without the Alien in the Robot's court he couldn't be certain of the Robot's role in everything that had happened. Medina had no cracks in his armor, either.

The Protector had returned to square one. On the long drive back to Crowsport, he'd wound the events backwards and started at the beginning. A Crowsport train, smuggling missiles out of Pallas, headed toward the ocean waterfront. There would be risk in starting the smuggling operation again, but only the Alien had known about the missiles. To the general public, and the authorities, the explosions had been the result of the train wreck. No one had made the connection to Medina's missing armaments.

Without the Alien in the way, smuggling would be easier.

In fact, without the Alien, why use Crowsport? Medina could go back to smuggling out of Pallas using methods from before the Alien had engaged in his crimefighting crusade.

It was time to sow the seeds of doubt.

There were two goons standing watch. If the Protector's guess was correct, their guard duty was a waste of time and money. He slipped through the gap in their predictable rotation and climbed up the access ladder at the rear of the first tanker. He didn't even need to reach the hatch to know his guess had been correct: his footsteps echoed inside the empty tank below.

"Hey! Who's there?" one of the goons challenged.

Powerful flashlight beams cut into the dark, searching haphazardly for the source of the noise. The lights played over the top of multiple tankers. The Protector had already backtracked to the ladder and slid down with hands and feet on the outside, avoiding the rungs.

Footsteps crunched gravel, thudded against dense wooden railroad ties. They were coming down a track toward the front of the tanker. He ran ahead to the next tanker car. He risked the exposure, sidled along the side of the tanker, and reached the end of it a second too late.

"There!"

A beam lit the Protector from behind, threw his shadow long. A shot rang out as he dove to the back of the tanker. He scrambled up to a sitting position behind the car.

The guards were being cautious. There was no shouting, no running. The Protector heard their footsteps, the slight grinding of soles against the hard ground. He heard the stifled breathing of a stealthy approach.

The Protector put on a set of brass knuckles. He rapped a fist against the tanker. The blows resounded in the hollow interior of the tanker car.

"Empty, too," the Protector muttered.

More shots were fired. The whine of bullets ricocheting off the steel tanker sang out. Gravel kicked up on his left and then on his right. Both toughs were firing sporadically—they wanted him pinned down until they reached him.

"Come out of there, you snoop!" one goon shouted. "You don't show yourself, and we aren't responsible if you catch a bullet!"

The Protector slipped off the brass knuckles and returned them to his pocket.

He could drop smoke bombs and then scale the fence. He could backtrack like a shadow in the night and return to the gap under the chain link. Or he might incapacitate both guards and then he could stroll out the main entrance. He could have escaped easily.

But that wasn't the Protector's plan.

He needed to try, though.

He tossed two smoke bombs, one to either side of the tanker car.

The Protector chose the left side and ran. He heard the coughing, the shuffling feet, saw the flashlight beam cut short in the thick smoke. Instead of running around the guard, he slammed headlong into the man. The Protector pushed the man's gun arm behind; it was pinned when they hit the ground.

Gun arm twisted under his back, the guard let go of the pistol rather than risk shooting himself in the scuffle. The Protector threw a few weak punches, the goon responded harder. The Protector kept moving so the hits were glancing blows. One punch slipped past, though, impacting his temple. He saw spots and stars for a moment. The brawler heaved up and rolled atop the Protector, trying to pin him down.

"I got 'im! I got 'im!" The gangster shouted over his shoulder. "Get over here! I got 'im!"

The Protector could have employed any number of maneuvers to dislodge the man. Instead, he squirmed under the weight. The other guard appeared and aimed his pistol at the Protector's head. The Protector stopped struggling. He put his hands over his head in surrender.

"It's the Protector," said the pistol man.

"Yeah. Caught us a big fish," replied the first goon. He glared down at the Protector. "You stayin' put?"

"I won't move a hair unless your friend with the gun says so."

The goon got to his feet and took a few steps backward until he was beside the armed man.

"Should we kill him?" the gunman asked.

"Probably. But the boss doesn't want any messes right now. I think we should keep him alive. We better ask the boss what he wants to do."

"Yeah," the Protector said. Despite the pummeling he had received, he flashed a smile. "Take me to your leader. I want to talk to him, anyway."

8. THE ROBOT UNDER ATTACK!

The Robot sat in the dark of the Lair, chin resting on tented fingers, data running through its mind. For a moment, it pulled back to study the pattern of its fingers and position of the hands. Why was it mimicking the Alien? It had no need to create a visual impression of deep thought, and yet it had.

It should have been continuing repairs and bringing systems online. The wireless connections were functional. It meant to replace the shattered panoramic window. The forcefield circuit needed repair. In the meantime, the penthouse sported wooden boards where its centerpiece view onto the world had been.

The Robot should have been preparing to undertake further investigation of Milton Medina, but it continued to ponder the Protector's accusations.

It leaned its chin back onto its tented fingers.

Had the Robot killed the Alien?

The Robot had tried to save the Alien. It had arrived too late. It had seen the Alien, briefly, and the strange energy; it had heard the odd sound.

Or had it?

Had the Robot's memory been altered? Had it altered its own memory? Was it suffering some sort of robot schizophrenia, unaware of a program lurking somewhere within?

The Protector believed the recent crimes were connected, but the Robot could not find logic in that deduction. If so, what would have possessed the Robot to break into the Moore-Rutledge observatory? Why would it steal Medina's laser? The Alien had been uneasy about the break-in. The Robot could not feel unease. The crime had no logical connection.

Had there been a retro-attack of some kind—a Trojan horse program—which had slipped past the Robot's defenses when it infiltrated the security system at Medina's factory?

The Robot would need to find a way to ensure its systems were clean and purged.

The Robot felt a jolt on its calf. Its leg was constructed of salvaged material from the Alien's pod. It was an extraterrestrial composite, light and extremely durable. It could withstand abuse. While not as sensitive as a layer of skin, it had sensors and transmitted data to the Robot's artificial brain.

The Robot looked down and saw two blue-green points of glowing diodes, eyes of some construct. The design was insectoid. It clung to the smooth leg via its own spidery appendages. The Robot saw an electrical spark arc between the robo-spider's mandibles before it zapped the leg again, leaving a short black scorch mark.

An audio-masked voice buzzed through the insect.

"Wireless infiltration is useful." The speaker sounded calm and clinical. "But sometimes, physical contact is required."

The Robot's internal audio system recorded the voice for later analysis. The Robot jumped to the conclusion that evidence would reveal Milton Medina's voice. An odd, illogical, and unsystematic thought.

The Robot reached down and plucked the mechanical bug from its leg, then scanned the robo-spider with various rendering abilities within its eye.

"Thank you for volunteering to participate in this field test," the voice said.

The Robot considered crushing the robo-spider between two fingers. It halted its planned destruction when it realized the communication might be two-way.

"Field test?" the Robot asked.

"These units will render you immobile. Then they will learn, adapt, and burrow into your shell." The voice maintained its clinical calmness. "Once inside, they should be able to access your systems."

The Robot cocked its head.

"Units?"

"Yes. You must have determined by now that a single construct would not have the capability to bring you down."

The Robot heard skittering; the sound seemed to come from everywhere at once. The floor lit blue-green as dozens of diode eyes gazed upward. The walls danced with pairs of scrambling eyes. The Robot turned its face to the ceiling, and more LEDs glared down.

The robo-spiders swarmed.

The mechanical insects spread over the Robot's body in a wave of bobbing lights and shiny metal carapaces. The Robot swept away swaths of the bugs, but the mechanical insects raced back, covering the Robot from head to toe. The robo-spiders bit all over. Though the Robot did not have a human sense of smell, its sensors reported scorched ozone.

No single bite penetrated the Robot's shell, but the sheer number of electric discharges distorted the Robot's sight and audio input. A cluster of the bugs clinging on the Robot's chest cascaded their amperage and voltage, as if attempting to reach a specific, congruent level. More joined the effort. Instead of their mandibles attacking the Robot's casing, the micro-jaws arced sparks and tendrils of electricity from one to the other. A web of crackling electricity flowed around the Robot, a net of energy.

The Robot tried to step away, but one of its legs would not move. The internal servo kept the knee from folding and spilling the Robot to the floor. Paralysis crept along the Robot's body.

The robo-spiders' electric net generated a powerful electromagnetic pulse. The surge of energy permeated the Robot's body. Systems blanked, went dormant. The Robot could no longer move under its own power. Algorithms and data separated, could not connect.

The Robot fought for clarity, triggering backup systems in its electronic brain. For a moment, it had a secondary route to access motor functions. How soon could the robo-spiders re-form the electromagnetic field?

The Robot considered vaulting out the window. It might survive the impact with the street and crush the spiders, but there might be pedestrians below.

Overanalyzing. Over extrapolating. Would the Alien stand

still and let a criminal punch while he considered his next action?

The Robot slapped its chest. A score of damaged bugs fell to the floor, legs flailing, carapaces cracked, electrical discharges arcing, LED eyes fading. Bugs shifted along the Robot's body, closing the gap in the electromagnetic web. The field was a weaker because the spiders were spread farther apart from each other.

The Robot grabbed the newly constructed wireless relay and tore it from its mooring, wires snapping. It tossed the unit across the room.

The spiders faltered. They continued to scramble and swarm, but they lacked a unified attack. Some fell off the Robot onto the floor, others continued their arcing bites on its body. The Robot stomped the floor, crushing the nuisances.

"A good try," the detached voice stated. The sound came through all the robo-spiders, giving it a strange buzzing quality, like sitting in the heart of a hornet nest. "Sending encrypted instructions over a public network carries too much risk of a breach."

The robo-spiders halted. Moments later, they again turned their pinpoint blue-green eyes toward the Robot. Cohesion returned to their collective. Again, they moved as a single entity.

"Who are you?" the Robot asked.

The mysterious voice declined to answer the question.

"You are extremely durable, if not invulnerable. Sometimes, a head-to-head confrontation is the least likely to succeed. A mouse to an elephant. A thorn in a lion's paw. Those are the success stories. Every Goliath has a David."

The Robot scanned as the robo-spiders ran up along its legs and torso, positioning to recreate their electric net. The Robot probed outward before they could emit another electromagnetic pulse. There had to be a form of communication controlling the robo-spiders. The Robot scanned spectrums and frequencies.

Shortwave signals!

The strength of the shortwave signals indicated the source was in close proximity to the penthouse lair. The Robot had been handed an unexpected advantage.

The Robot beat its chest, destroying more of the insect units. Before more could swarm, the Robot leapt and smashed through the boarded panoramic window. Wood splintered and cracked. The Robot's flight system engaged. There was still the danger of shutting down and crashing onto the street below.

The spiders no longer had reinforcements leaping from the walls or dropping from the ceiling. They tenaciously clung to the Robot's carapace. Another electromagnetic pulse was developing, cascading through the mechanical bugs. They would strike in moments.

The Robot homed in on the source of the shortwave broadcast. Engaging the boosters in the soles of its feet, the Robot curved its trajectory around the corner edge of a skyscraper.

The source was dead ahead.

The hovering gyrocopter was surprisingly quiet. Its rotors cut through the air in silence, and the efficient engine hummed softly. The pilot wore a full flight helmet, obscuring their face, but the form-fitting leather jumpsuit highlighted the physique of a woman. The height to which her knees were drawn up in the little craft's seat indicated she was tall.

The Robot wondered if she was the one talking. The word choice seemed more aligned with Medina. He might be speaking from afar, while she operated the robo-spiders at closer range.

A surge of electricity ran through the web of robo-spiders. The electromagnetic pulse created random failures throughout the Robot. The Robot's boosters faltered and shut down. It lost use of its left arm. Its vision was impaired thirty percent. The anti-gravity unit remained online, keeping it in the air.

The Robot flew at the gyrocopter.

The pilot spun the craft and retreated.

Even without boosters, the Robot gained on the gyrocopter. The pilot glanced back over her shoulder. The Robot could not calculate if it could catch her before the next pulse from the spiders struck.

Smoke puffed from tubes under the seat of the gyrocopter. Two rockets sped toward the Robot.

The Robot's first protocol response was to maneuver away from harm. It overrode its defaults and waited. Internal systems sent warnings. The Robot ignored them. It took the risk, not knowing the power of the explosives in the rocket heads. The Robot could withstand powerful physical impacts, but it had never field tested its own body against the same levels of abuse the Alien had experienced.

The rockets exploded in front of the Robot. The shockwave knocked the Robot through the air. Explosive residue burned on its body, leaving a smoking trail through the sky. The explosion dislodged most of the robo-spiders.

The Robot analyzed its damage: superficial. Shrapnel scratches and scorch marks. The shockwave had not affected its internal systems.

The gyrocopter continued its retreat. Systems recovered; the Robot fired its boosters. Its red-highlighted black body raced toward its attacker. More rockets fired from the rear of the gyrocopter. The sky filled with smoke and thunder. The Robot maneuvered through the explosions, but shockwaves shoved it off course. It wasn't much of a deflection, but it gave the pilot a few moments to increase her distance.

The small sky-craft angled down and away. It flitted past buildings, skirting dangerously close to walls. The Robot glanced toward the ground, saw automobiles and people moving, though some were stopping in their tracks and pointing upward, including heads protruding from car windows. The pilot might have hoped to lure the Robot into a crash, but the Robot put concern for citizens and property before a tight pursuit.

The gyrocopter flew toward the lapping waves of Mighty Lake. Continuing its descent, the craft's running lights went out as it passed into dark alleys and city shadows. Silent and dark, the machine's stealth might have confounded any other pursuer, but the Robot followed. The craft created a heat signature, augmented by the chill night air.

Flying high enough to clear a perimeter fence, the gyrocopter sped to a sectioned-off parcel of shoreline. Ahead, a lake freighter lay berthed, and the craft alighted on the deck of the ship. The pilot leapt out of gyrocopter. She ran toward the smaller superstructure built over the bow.

The Robot's quarry had access to the ship's interior. There was no hesitation attempting to breach the lock. She knew the access code. As the Robot landed on the deck, the access door swung shut.

The Robot predicted ownership of the vessel would trace back to Medina. Securing the capture of the attacker would provide better evidence of a connection.

The Robot strode across the deck, past the closed cargo hatches. The security system was simple. The Robot entered the correct access code within moments. The lock clicked open and the red light switched to green.

The Robot hesitated, recalling the death of the Alien—a diversionary attack followed by a trap. Cautiously, the Robot proceeded. It scanned for any wireless signal usage. If the pilot had a communications device wired into her flight helmet, she was not currently in contact with anyone outside.

The cavernous steel vessel was far from ideal for a stealthy search. The Robot could not prevent its heavy footfalls from echoing. The pilot would hear.

But not if the Robot flew.

Engaging its anti-gravity unit, the Robot lifted a few inches above the floor. There were two staircases. The one on the left ascended into the superstructure above. The right staircase led down, into the bowels of the ship.

A clatter—quickly stifled—came from the descending stairwell.

The Robot followed the sound. At the bottom of the staircase, a metal hatchway opened into a long corridor dotted with further hatches, all hanging open. A few lamps on clip hangers and spotlight stands threw harsh light and dark shadows. The lack of crew led the Robot to consider whether the vessel was under repair or derelict.

Along the line of sight down the corridor, the Robot saw the fleeing pilot. She had removed her helmet—it was too dark, and a lack of peripheral vision in the compressed space would be a problem. The beam from a handheld light bobbed as she ran in the dark. She lost time stepping through each undersized entrance way.

The Robot leaned into a prone flying position and shot down the passage.

Glancing over her shoulder, the pilot spotted the Robot. She slammed shut the next door she passed. The hatchway wheel spun. It would not stop the Robot, but it would delay pursuit. As the Robot opened the door, it heard more hatches slamming shut farther down the passageway.

The Robot pursued, losing time to open each closed hatch. It traversed the belly of the lake freighter and reached the stern of the craft. The Robot glided up the stairwell and paused at the top. Had the fleeing pilot gone up into the stern superstructure? There would be a labyrinth of places to hide—crew quarters, galley, bridge. Her only hope would be for the Robot to pass her so she could double back. Her chances of detection were high.

More likely, she would try to return to the gyrocopter.

The Robot stepped out onto the main deck.

The woman leapt from behind the tall lip of the nearest cargo bay.

"Hold this!"

Something squeezed onto the Robot's hand. It looked down and saw a clamp on its hand wired to a box device.

The tip of an arc welder stabbed against the Robot's throat.

There was a flash and smoke. The Robot staggered back a step, but its outer casing was not as metallic as it appeared. It did not conduct electricity efficiently, but the crossed circuit of the arc caused a distracting level of damage.

Like a boxer taking a punch, the Robot shook its head. It pulled the clamp off its hand, crushing the metal pincers.

The pilot ran along the deck, headed for the gyrocopter.

Someone leapt out from behind another cargo lid and tackled the fleeing woman. They rolled on the deck, but the pilot broke her assailant's hold. The two fighters faced off, and then spun into kicks and counterpunches.

Forgetting flight for the moment, the Robot ran toward the combatants. Heat signatures weren't any use for identification, but heightened vision revealed the pilot's attacker wore an aviator's cap and goggles. The Robot increased its speed, but by the time it reached the struggle, it was too late.

The woman was waiting for him. Without her helmet, the Robot recognized the short cropped red hair from surveillance photographs. She was Milton Medina's personal assistant, Josephine Kinney.

Holding a pistol in one hand, Josephine had her left elbow locked around the Understudy's neck. The Robot knew the Understudy was versed in physical and martial abilities, but with the gun at her head she dared not move.

"No closer." Josephine waved the pistol briefly at the Robot and quickly repositioned the gun's aim at the Understudy's head.

The Robot looked beyond the fence, where a motorcycle had been parked under the flickering, dim light attached to the power pole. The motorcycle was unregistered and flaunted a style reminiscent of the Protector's favored custom automobile. Deep in the bowels of the ship, the Robot had not heard the Understudy's arrival.

"I thought you returned to Crowsport with the Protector," the Robot said.

"I wasn't finished here yet," the Understudy said. "I didn't know where to find you, so I went to the Lair. I got there just in time to see your dogfight in the sky. Thought I'd follow,"

"Why?" the Robot asked.

"Thought I might need to rescue you," the Understudy said. "Sorry."

"Lucky me. This young lady should help bring our little chase to an end now." Josephine squeezed her elbow a little tighter, eliciting a strangled gasp from the Understudy. "Turn off whatever you're recording."

Josephine shoved the barrel of the pistol against the Understudy's temple.

"Five, four, three...."

"Done." The Robot held out its hands, trying to calm the situation. "Do not do anything rash, please."

"Now, erase it all. The chase, the gyrocopter, this conversation." Josephine showed her teeth in a grim smile. "Five...."

"There is no need to count," the Robot interrupted. "The data has been removed."

"You swear?"

"I am a robot. I cannot make oaths, but I cannot lie, either."

"All right." Josephine grinned. "I guess this is the part where we parley."

"Let her go," the Robot said. "And I will let you go."

"Is that a promise?"

"Yes."

"If you can't make oaths, you can't make promises, either." Josephine shuffled two steps backward, dragging the Understudy with her. "I'm afraid I can't accept that arrangement."

"Then what do you suggest?"

"Leave."

"I won't leave without her. That is an arrangement I cannot accept."

Josephine surveyed their surroundings. Her gaze settled upward, looking at the bright red lifeboat above their heads. The lifeboat was an enclosed capsule—more like a short submarine, though it was not designed for submerging.

She indicated the stairs with a toss of her head. "Up there. You first. Walk, no flying."

The Robot clanked up the metal steps. Josephine kept a tight grip on the Understudy, gun firmly pressed against her back.

"One wrong move," Josephine said.

"Got it," the Understudy said.

The two women followed the Robot up the stairs. They reached the berth of the lifeboat. Designed for a free fall into the water, the bullet-shaped craft was little more than an oversized canister. It sat at an angle, ready to plunge into the water upon release. It had one entrance—a hatch at the rear.

"Open it," Josephine said.

The Robot complied. The interior of the lifeboat was stark: benches with compartments underneath, and an uncomfortable looking seat for the pilot. Safety belts hung along the walls. There were bulbous windows at the prow and along the sides.

"Back away."

The Robot moved away from the hatch. Josephine maneuvered her captive closer to the lifeboat. At the open hatch, keeping her pistol aimed at the Understudy's head, Josephine pulled a zip tie from a pocket. She lashed the Understudy's wrists and stepped away, out of range of punches or kicks. She kept her gun trained on the young woman.

"Get in."

The Understudy hesitated. She glanced at the Robot. The Robot nodded that she should proceed. It thought to rush and put its body between the gun and the Understudy, but decided against the attempt. It would not be fast enough. Josephine would pull the trigger before the Robot could be in position. The Robot had formidable strength and endurance, but it did not have super-speed.

Reluctantly, the Understudy climbed into the open lifeboat. She almost tripped over the edge of the doorway. She recovered her balance despite the added challenge of her wrists being bound.

"Sit there, at the end of the bench," Josephine instructed. "Do not step out of my line of sight, or I shoot."

The Understudy sat, lifted her arms, and held onto a belt to keep from sliding farther down the bench.

Keeping her gun and eyes trained on the Understudy, Josephine spoke to the Robot.

"You understand how this works?" She cocked her head to indicate the lifeboat.

"I accessed manuals and schematics as we approached," the Robot answered. "A free-fall lifeboat. Once safety pins are removed, and the crew safely aboard, the pilot pulls a release from inside."

"It can be done from outside, too." Josephine nodded at the Robot. "Pull the release pins. Move very slowly or I shoot her."

The Robot complied. From either side of the metal framework around the lifeboat, it removed the pins. Mechanical latches clicked free. Metal groaned and cables whined. The Understudy gave a startled cry.

"Oh, you're not going anywhere yet," Josephine said. "The main lashing is still holding on."

"Why are you doing this?" the Robot asked.

"Walk over to the railing and take a good look down," Josephine said to the Robot.

The Robot did. The freighter had berthed prow first. Given the length of the vessel, standing on the stern, they jutted out into the lake. Below, the water was deep. It had to be, or the freighter would have run aground.

Josephine placed her hand on a metal arm attached to the safely cable holding the main lashing in place.

"It's a bad idea to launch a lifeboat into the water with the hatch wide open."

"Stop," the Robot said.

"Save her or catch me." Josephine pulled the handle. The main lashing slipped away. "Your choice, Robot."

The lifeboat slipped from its deck-side mooring and plummeted. The Understudy screamed. The boat hit the lake, bobbed up momentarily, and then the chill water flooded into the open hatchway.

9. ON THE RUN

The fall happened so fast, and yet time seemed to stand still. The Understudy could not move fast enough. She thought she could latch herself into a seatbelt before the lifeboat hit the water, but with her wrists bound the task was more difficult. It seemed the belt dragged across her chest like a languid python. She shoved the latch plate down and missed, the seatbelt did not lock.

The lifeboat impacted the surface of the lake, nose down. She was tossed forward. She tightened her grip on the belt, but it wasn't enough. Gravity pulled hard. She lost her hold, fell into the nose of the craft. She hit the pilot's seat, spun, and impacted the windows over the bow. The boat bobbed up, she rolled and landed hard on the floor.

She gasped in pain. Every muscle in her back had twisted into a knot. The back of her skull ached. She would have screamed, but water rushed over her and took her breath away. Between her injuries and the zip tie around her wrists, she floundered. She could not stand up. Water spilled in through the open hatch.

The Understudy got to her knees. She shuffled forward, pulling herself along the edges of the seats, her knees aching as they ground against the wet metal floor.

The lifeboat lurched. The water reversed direction. It ran away from her, spilling out the stern. She slipped, following the flow, but grabbed hold of a seat belt. She realized the slight tilted angle to the craft was just enough to evacuate the water. There was no danger of slipping out, she'd be caught on the lip of the hatchway.

There was the sensation of movement. The lifeboat was in motion. She stared uncomprehendingly at the lights blurring past the windows.

The boat was flying!

The flight lasted for a few moments before she heard twisting, grinding metal. The hull scraped against dry land. The boat stopped, rolled to the left side of its keel.

The Robot appeared in the hatchway.

"Are you all right?"

Relief flooded over the Understudy. She found she could say nothing. She nodded instead.

The Robot held a twist of metal in its hand. It seemed to notice the metal only when the Understudy looked at it quizzically.

"I lifted the boat from the water. The sprinkler piping along the top exterior was the quickest method of getting a grip." The Robot tossed away the pipe. "It is not designed for weight bearing, though."

The Robot hunched, preparing to climb into the boat. She held out her palms.

"I can move. Just give me a minute."

"We only have twenty-five seconds."

The Understudy grunted in frustration. She scrambled until she was standing. She didn't move so much as she forced her body forward by any means necessary. She ignored her pain. She didn't know the reason for the urgency, but she did not doubt the Robot's word.

"What now? A time bomb?"

The Robot shook its head. When she was within reach, the Robot pulled her out of the boat. They were on the strand not too far away from the freighter. The Robot pointed to specks of red light in the sky.

"Incoming."

The gyrocopter.

Flames flashed and smoke enveloped the red lights.

The Robot and the Understudy ran.

The rockets hit the beached lifeboat. One shot flew into the open hatch. The interior lit up as the boat danced, briefly lifted off the ground, and settled again.

The Understudy peered around the Robot. The explosions had dented and smashed the vessel. It looked like a can which had imploded and exploded at the same time. If she had been in the boat, she would have been pulverized. It was not a comforting thought.

She looked for the gyrocopter. The red lights were receding.

"Will she come around for another pass?"

"I think not. She attempted one more attack without engaging me directly. I am not sure how many rockets she had left. Those might have been her last."

The Understudy sighed and sank to her knees. She closed her eyes, sucked in air through her nostrils, and blew the chill air out through her mouth. She wasn't out of the fight, but she needed a moment to recuperate.

"Now you can go catch her."

"No." The Robot crouched beside the Understudy and broke the zip tie around her wrists. "I think we should stay together right now. Perhaps you can answer my question."

She closed her eyes. She felt bumps and bruises welling up on her back and her head.

"What question?"

"Why are you still here in Pallas? I assumed you had returned to Crowsport with the Protector."

"We had an argument."

"I am assuming you have arguments all the time."

"We do." The Understudy looked up into the Robot's face. "But this was a big one. An important one."

"About me?"

"Yes. Good deduction. About you."

"He told you his theory—that I killed the Alien?"

"I don't believe what he believes."

The Understudy tried to stand. Her resolve dissipated. She decided she would wait another moment.

"I appreciate your confidence in my innocence," the Robot said.

"I think Medina's hellcat attacking you should be proof enough. If he had control over you, there'd be easier ways to get rid of you."

The Understudy's adrenaline was spent. Her head throbbed, competing with her back in a contest of which could create the most distracting pain. Exhaustion blanketed every fiber of her body.

"Hey," the Understudy said.

"Yes?"

"I'm not so impervious as you." The Understudy shivered. "In fact, I'm rather beat up and probably getting close to hypothermia. If you want to keep talking, take me someplace warm and dry."

The Understudy awoke. She regretted it immediately. The muscles of her back were knotted and sore. Her head had a dull ache, but she could move it to either side without wooziness. She closed her eyes and then registered something she had seen. She opened her eyes.

Tinted glass surrounded her. A dome. They were flying. Sunrise peeked through the buildings ahead. She recognized the skyline of Crowsport. The Robot sat in the seat beside her, arms gripping a steering wheel. A dashboard laid out in a semi-circle around them. The vents were blasting hot air.

Earlier—before she had almost collapsed from her ordeal—the Robot had flown her through the streets of Pallas. She did not remember falling asleep.

"Where are we?"

"In the Alien's hover-car."

"Hover? We're hundreds of feet above the ground!"

"He made adjustments to the vehicle." The Robot seemed to shrug—or tried to. "I suppose you would consider it to be a flying car. Like you might see on old science fiction magazine covers."

"A flying car?" The Understudy looked around the dome, at the city ahead and the sky above. She craned her neck to look down past the edge of the bottom half of the craft. "But you can fly. The Alien could fly. Why do you need a flying car?"

"Transport." The Robot held out its hand and spread its fingers. "There is only so much surface area. There is a limit to how much can be carried by hand—regardless of strength."

The Understudy turned and viewed the rear of the hover-car. The hover-car had an oversized trunk molded into the body. The airborne vehicle could haul its share as well as any automobile.

"Neither of you would need heat, though."

"True. But a passenger might."

The fog lifting from her awareness, the Understudy noticed the chattering of various audio sources. She heard snippets of police dispatches, news broadcasts, various podcasts, different languages. She didn't know how many speakers were hooked up inside the car, but the cacophony threatened to bring on a headache.

"Can your passenger opt out of all that noise?"

"Certainly," replied the Robot. Its spindly fingers ran over a set of knobs and buttons.

The blathering channels went silent. A quiet classical score played gently. The music matched the beauty of the rising sun. In contrast, the streets and buildings of Crowsport radiated a grim doom, even in the increasing morning light.

"I thought you would take me back to the Lair."

"The Lair is compromised. I have no other place. I thought the hover-car would be the best option. We are safe. You can rest while we proceed to Crowsport."

"Why Crowsport?"

"To return you home."

Chagrined, the Understudy crossed her arms.

"I was going to help you. I don't need to be chaperoned home."

"You can help. But you need rest. I had nowhere to offer you to stay in Pallas."

The Understudy gave the Robot the benefit of the doubt. At least he hadn't treated her like a child.

"You should talk to the Protector while you are here. Now that Medina went after you, he must believe you. I can vouch for you."

"I agree. Where will we find him?"

They had crossed over from the suburbs to the sprawl of neighborhoods within the city limits. The skyscrapers of downtown loomed ahead. Despite being Crowsport born and bred, the city frightened the Understudy as much as it thrilled her. Trying to take it all in from the air was overwhelming. What could she and the Protector do against all the evil that wormed through those streets and buildings? There were good people in the city, too, she reminded herself. They were worth helping and protecting.

"We're going to need to ditch the car, it's sure to attract attention. Secret identity and all that. Can't advertise where we hide out."

"Of course. I never had to deal with that aspect of the Alien's existence. He was known to all."

"Hard to hide when you're green and tall."

"Or a robot. Hiding this vehicle might not be enough to dissuade attention."

The Understudy cocked her head.

"Good point." She had started to think of the Robot as another person, despite its appearance. "We'll use one of the safehouses. The Protector has them scattered around the city. If we're noticed, it will only be the loss of one hideout. Head to the left."

The Robot navigated the hover-car over short buildings and maneuvered past the taller ones.

"Bring it down over there." The Understudy pointed at the flat top of a tall building. Dull green metal structures dotted the roof. "Those HVAC units will give some cover."

The hover-car came down on the roof with the finesse of a feather on the wind. Nestled between two oversized green unit housings, it seemed safe enough. The Understudy scanned the skies for news or police helicopters. After a few moments, she was satisfied. No telling what anyone on the street might have seen or reported, though. The Robot and the Understudy disembarked. They tried the door to the stairs into the building, but it was locked.

"Shall we force it?"

"No. Let's not attract any more attention than we already have." The Understudy glanced around. It was early morning; the city was coming to life. "I wonder if anyone saw us."

"If curiosity does bring someone up here, the car cannot go anywhere without its key."

"I didn't see a key."

"I am the key." The Robot walked to the edge of the roof and peered down at the alley below.

The Understudy swung a leg over the short wall. The Robot seemed to stare at her.

"What?"

"Shall I carry you down?" the Robot asked.

"I hadn't thought of that." The Understudy pulled her leg off the wall. "Force of habit. I was going to climb down the fire escape."

The Robot held the Understudy and stepped over the edge. Rather than a swooping, flying pattern, the Robot simply descended in a straight line. The sensation felt the same as an elevator ride.

Leading the Robot, the Understudy kept to alleys and morning shadows. She felt like a fugitive on the run. She kept looking to the sky, half-expecting the gyrocopter to swoop down. Maybe the thought wasn't completely irrational. Medina had private jets. He could have sent Josephine to Crowsport. She could have arrived before they had. Would she have brought the gyrocopter if that were the case?

How much did Medina need the Robot out of the way? Enough to pursue them to Crowsport? Or would it be enough that the Robot had left Pallas—at least, temporarily?

A few blocks away from the building where they had stashed the hover-car, a wooden fence surrounded a small area. The Understudy walked to the side of the lot. She glanced around for onlookers. Satisfied there were none, she pressed her palm against a specific post. A section of fence slid aside.

An old building constructed of stone and brick loomed over the grounds. Marble stairs led to the front entrance, where a columned cornice perched over a set of large wooden doors. In one window, a faded sign proclaimed: *BOOKS ARE BETTER!*

"A library," the Robot said.

"It had been a neighborhood branch of the city library. They let it go some years ago."

The Understudy unlocked the door. Books were strewn on the floor and remaining wood-framed chairs. No one had bothered to remove the library materials. Along with the neglected and vandalized books, long out-of-date flyers and announcements were pinned to old cork boards. The library hadn't been so much closed as it had been abandoned without a proper shutdown.

"Don't mind the appearance. It's supposed to look like squatters live here or, at least, to look like people have slipped in from time to time. It helps the cover." The Understudy bent down and scooped up a book. She thumbed through it, showing the Robot the blank pages. "The Protector moved out the real books. He couldn't see them go to waste."

She led the Robot past the desk.

"Come on. The staff room is the real hideout. It's in good shape."

They entered a stairwell on the right. On the second floor, the Understudy unlocked a door. In the large room, an empty coffee maker and a microwave oven were on the short counter along the back wall. The counter also had a sink, above and below which were pantry doors. The chairs and central table were in good condition. The floor was clean. The Understudy sagged into a seat and rubbed her head.

"Are you all right?" the Robot asked.

"Tired. Sore. But, yeah. All right."

She rested for a minute, then got out of her seat and opened a cabinet. She prepared coffee. While her brew heated up, she poured some breakfast cereal into a bowl.

"I'm guessing you don't need food." The Understudy crunched a mouthful. She was too hungry to wait for a hot meal, despite the microwave oven. She slurped her coffee. It wasn't proper coffee from a shop, but the aroma was a comfort.

"Do you have means of contacting the Protector from here?"

"He knows. I tripped a proximity alarm downstairs. I'm surprised he's not here already."

The Robot turned toward the window.

"Someone is."

"I was joking." The Understudy leapt from her chair.

"Unless he happened to be in the neighborhood, he couldn't get here that fast."

Outside, three black limousines had pulled to the curb. Men in two-piece suits stepped out, dark glasses on their faces and guns in hand. Some held pistols; two, at least, had shotguns. One went around to the trunk and pulled out a long black case. The Understudy suspected it held a rocket launcher.

Someone else reached into the trunk and pulled out a chainsaw. The Understudy wondered if they had known there was a wooden fence. Or were they the kind of criminals who used chainsaws for worse things, and kept one handy in the trunk? The man jerked on the pull cord. The engine roared. The teeth of the blade bit into the wood slats of the fence.

"We've been compromised," the Robot said.

"Yes. But how?" The Understudy chugged the coffee remaining in her cup. She didn't have time for savoring.

The Robot cocked its head as if listening for something. It straightened its neck and reached out a hand. Mechanical fingers plucked at the back of Understudy's coat. The Robot held up a button-sized object. The Understudy could see the adhesive residue on the black metal.

"Tracer." The Robot crushed the device between its finger and its thumb.

"It must have been her—the pilot. Stuck it on my back when she grabbed me."

"Her name is Josephine Kinney."

"Yeah, her." The Understudy looked out the window again. "I don't see her out there."

"Medina doesn't need to send her," the Robot said. "He can contract out to Dufresne's organization here in Crowsport."

"Weapons cache."

The Understudy vaulted across the table. She opened a pantry door over the sink. Inside, an array of weapons hung on pegs. The Understudy chose a telescoping baton from the miscellaneous collection of shuriken, nunchaku, and other hand-to-hand weapons.

"Do you want something?"

The Robot scanned the small armory.

"These are all hand-held weapons. I do not have your dexterity."

The Understudy opened the next door to the left. Another array of weapons was on display. There were various non-lethal handguns. Some were regular guns loaded with rubber bullets. Others were higher tech.

"What about a missile weapon?"

"I am a missile," the Robot said.

"Sure. But sometimes it's better to keep your distance—even for you."

She handed the Robot an oversized black pistol with a large rectangular barrel.

The Robot hefted the weapon, turning it in its hand as it examined the gun.

"What does it use as a projectile?"

"Shockwaves. Small, concentrated. Should knock most anyone down hard." The Understudy held up three fingers. "But you've only got three rounds, and it takes time to spool up in between."

They were halfway down the stairs when the front doors exploded inward. Small-caliber slugs tore into the lobby. Books exploded in flurries of shredded paper, glass shattered, and wood splintered. After the initial flurry of madness, the guns went silent.

"They're done softening us up." The Understudy's baton telescoped out from her hand. "Cover me."

The Understudy leapt down over the remaining stairs, not waiting for a protest from the Robot. She somersaulted across the lobby floor, arriving at the wall beside the shattered double doors.

Her heart hammered in her chest. She tried not to think about her baton versus the firepower waiting outside. Knives, clubs, and fists were manageable. She wondered how the Protector had ever gotten so nonchalant when the criminals were shooting in his direction. She needed to add that trick to her training.

The first gangster stalked through the door, sweeping his pistol from side to side. The Understudy's baton came down hard, breaking a wrist bone. His yelp was cut short when the baton snapped against his chin, spinning him into the doorframe. Blood gushed from his smashed nose and lips.

The second attacker stepped over the jamb. Something whined and popped. The Understudy felt the wisp of warm air as a shockwave went past her and slammed into the intruder's belly. He doubled over and flew back out the door. Some of the others had bunched up behind, and the cluster of gangsters went down like bowling pins.

The Robot crossed the lobby and paused at the doors.

"On second thought," the Robot handed her the shockwave gun. "I believe we will reach a resolution more quickly if you cover me."

The Understudy nodded in agreement. Heroics had their place, but she might get killed in this fight. The Robot was an excellent shield.

The Robot marched out the door. Gunfire erupted again, but none of the slugs halted the Robot's advance. One man was armed with a machine pistol. He concentrated his rapid fire at the Robot's chest. The Robot surged forward. The man screamed in frustration at the ineffectuality of his weapon. He was still shouting when the Robot crushed the gun in its grip and tossed the man aside.

"Back off."

The order came from one of two men who had taken firing positions behind the limousines. The Robot advanced. The criminals closest to the building retreated. One of the men ran to the trunk of the car. He pulled out another rocket launcher and hurriedly prepped the weapon.

The Understudy knew the rocket would not cause any more damage to the Robot than the slugs had, but she refused to be an idle bystander. Kneeling behind a stone column at the entrance, she took aim. The shockwave pistol pulsed. The range to the rocket shooter was too far for full effect, but the force was enough. The man staggered back. The launcher triggered. The rocket went wide, exploding against the building somewhere overhead. Chunks of masonry rained down, bounced off the cornice, and danced to the ground.

Over the ringing in her ears, the Understudy heard a growling, sputtering sound. An engine roared. The chainsaw wielder charged at her from around the corner of the building.

The shockwave pistol hadn't spooled its next charge. She leaned left. The chainsaw bucked off the column. Shards of marble spat out where the blade chewed into the stone. The next downward swipe was too close. She leapt back and swung the barrel of her gun. It deflected the blade, but the teeth tore open her pistol. The Understudy tossed the ruined gun away and readied her baton.

It was terrifying to be on the other end of the spinning saw teeth. Even a glancing blow could tear meat from her body in a hideous wound, but the chainsaw was awkward to wield. Her attacker swung the tool in haphazard sweeps. She dodged, ducked into a squat, brought her leg around and tripped her opponent. He fell toward the churning chainsaw blade and screamed in terror. He eased his grip off the trigger as he fell and landed on the saw. Lucky for him, the chain had stopped moving before his stomach pressed against it.

The Understudy rapped his fingers hard with the baton and struck hard blows to his ankles to keep him temporarily hobbled. She rolled him off the chainsaw, swept it up in one hand and shoved the tip of the blade against his cheek, letting a sawtooth prick his skin.

"You're lucky I don't have the time for this now," the Understudy told the whimpering man. She unscrewed the fuel cap and tossed the chainsaw into the brush on the edge of the property.

Three attackers remained. They hustled into one limousine. The Robot sprinted across the gap to the car. It stood in front of the vehicle. The car lurched forward. The Robot bent over, caught the impact, and slipped its hands beneath the bumper. The Robot lifted the front of the car. The front tires spun in the air, the drive wheel useless. The Robot flipped the limousine over onto its roof.

The Understudy surveyed the carnage. The men were either unconscious, dazed, or groaning and flailing. Through the blasted front doors there were smoke and flames. The first rocket had ignited the books. The blaze was spreading.

She heard sirens in the distance.

"We should get going to the next safehouse." The Understudy trotted across the lawn to the Robot. "We don't want to be tangled up in a police investigation."

The Robot squatted down to check on the men in the car. There was movement but no one started any more shooting.

"We do not require the safehouse now," the Robot said. "We have a bigger problem."

"Like what?"

The Robot wrenched open the limousine door and reached in. The men inside hollered in panic, but the Robot did not grab any of them. It pulled something out and held it in front of the Understudy.

Though the object in the Robot's hand was beaten and crushed, there was no mistaking the Protector's fedora.

10. INSIDE THE FACTORY

The accommodations were what the Protector expected. From the echoes, he surmised he was in a cavernous, nondescript warehouse. They had him blindfolded, but he knew it was night. They must have had lights on. He could sense the glare. They roughly shoved him into an uncomfortable bare metal chair.

The blindfold was pulled from his eyes. He blinked at the brightness until his pupils adjusted. The goon squad were eyeing him. To a man, they were uniformed in suits and ties with bulges of pistol butts under their arms, or in their waistbands. Standing a head shorter but wider than any of his men, Charles Dufresne's corpulent face sneered at the Protector.

"You have some nerve telling my guys you want to talk to me." The mobster huffed his chest out and shrugged. "Like I should waste my time with you. I should've just phoned it in and told them to kill you."

"I do want to talk with you." The Protector shook his head. "And you probably want to hear what I have to say."

"Maybe you're yapping to stay alive," Dufresne said. "You were poking around my railroad. You got sloppy. My guys nabbed you, fair and square. Maybe if you tell me something I don't know, I'll let you off."

"I don't get the fancy restaurant treatment like Medina?"
Dufresne grunted.
"So, you want to talk about him? Okay, smart guy. Talk."

The Protector grinned. He'd scouted Dufresne's rail yards and found the empty tanker cars. Given Dufresne's surly attitude when the Protector mentioned Medina, the Protector knew he was on the right track.

"I decided to...do a little homework, Dufresne." The Protector wanted to kick out his legs and cross his feet. He scanned the faces in the room. He knew asking for release from his bonds would be futile. "You see, I'm trying to figure out what you are going to do with all your empty tanker cars. Where's the cargo you're waiting for?"

"Delay is all," the mobster answered. "What makes you think they're going to stay empty?"

"You think Medina is going to bother using you now that the Alien is dead? He can go back to smuggling straight out of Pallas, like he used to."

The mobster shrugged and feigned disinterest.

"It's a free country. We ain't signed a contract."

"Criminals never sign contracts, Dufresne. We both know that. Paper trails are bad for business. You had an agreement." The Protector tsk-tsked. "You're going to lose a big customer. I wonder why you're not fighting harder about it."

"We do lots of business without him. Medina isn't as big a piece of the pie as you might think."

"No. Certainly not. Not with you giving him such a deep discount on your service—a coerced discount, the way I hear it."

"What do you hear?"

"Oh no. I've talked enough. This is the good stuff. I'm not giving it away for free."

Dufresne looked at one of his men and cocked his head to indicate the Protector. The enforcer stepped forward. He cuffed the Protector across the cheek. It hurt, but the Protector knew the man had held back. If the goon let loose, it would be a painful conversation.

"Talk!" Dufresne demanded.

The Protector shook his head but didn't let his discomfort show.

"You all have guns. You've stripped me down. Cut me loose first. My hands and feet are going numb."

"All right," said Dufresne. "Cover him."

The gangsters pulled their guns, trained them on the Protector.

"One move. Just one...." Dufresne threatened. He waved at

another goon: tall, with a cleft lip. The man flashed a butterfly knife and cut through the ropes.

The Protector stayed seated. He stretched his legs and rubbed his wrists.

"What do you know about my arrangement with Medina?" Dufresne asked.

"He's got information on you. I know where he got it."

"And you're just going to tell me?"

"Yes."

"You must be working an angle." The gangster rubbed his jowls.

"What does it matter to you, if you get what you want?"

"I don't trust you."

"You don't need to." The Protector waved at Dufresne's men and their pointed guns. "Will you let me go if what I tell you is useful?"

"Maybe." The mob boss wasn't about to promise anything.

The Protector drew an audible breath.

"Alan Stumper."

Dufresne's eyes bulged.

"Stumper's dead!"

"That's what you're supposed to believe. That's the only reason the goods Medina had on you didn't ring a bell in your head. You didn't bother to check for the obvious."

The information had some effect on the hard-nosed crime boss. He paced in front of the Protector's chair, his composure giving way to rising anger.

"Stumper's alive?"

"Until a few days ago. He'd been under an assumed name—and Medina's protection."

Dufresne gnawed his lip.

"What happened to him?"

The Protector gave a wry smile. "He was—I believe the phrase is—hoisted on his own petard."

"That son of a...."

"I told you I had useful information."

Dufresne shook his fist at the Protector.

"All right, I'm done pussyfooting around with Medina.

Thinks he's so smooth. Mister Business. Mister Public. No one knows what he really is." Dufresne thumped on his chest. "Well, I know what he is. And he ain't half the tough guy he thinks."

"Might I suggest a visit to his factory on the outskirts of Pallas? The one on Frontage Avenue," the Protector said. "He's got something extra secret going on there. You might find him there if you're lucky. If not, he'll come running. Easier than trying to get him at home or at the office."

"Thanks for the tip. You really got it in for him, eh? Why?"

"You and I both know he had the Alien murdered—even if he didn't do it himself."

The mob boss nodded.

"Saddle up," Dufresne waved his hand in a circle. "We're taking a trip to Pallas."

The Protector rose slowly from the chair.

"Not you," Dufresne said. "Sit down."

"I'm not invited?" The Protector dropped back in the seat.

"I won't have room in the trunk for a body, on account of all the guns we'll be bringing."

"Breaking a truce." The Protector shook his head. "Not good for your reputation."

Dufresne laughed. "You're not going to be alive to tell anyone, smart guy. Truces with guys on the other side of the law don't count."

The Protector folded his arms and brought his feet together. "Can't say I'm surprised."

They had removed the Protector's coat and hat. They had torn open his shirt to check for a holstered pistol under his arm.

They hadn't considered his shoes. Unnoticed, the Protector rubbed the sides of the heels together.

A cloud of smoke spewed from the sparking of his shoes; each side coated with a complementary incendiary chemical. The Protector sprawled on the floor. Pistols bucked and slugs riddled the chair. He sprang to his feet and uppercut the nearest tough.

The Protector tackled another opponent around the knees. He delivered stunning blows to the man's head. The Protector retreated, but he didn't have much cover. The warehouse was large and stark, but the cloud of smoke was small and centralized. It would dissipate soon. It had been the last trick he had available.

The Protector heard running feet that were not shod in the gangsters' typical hard-soled shoes. He heard punches landing with muted thuds. Something sounded like machinery in motion, but he didn't hear an engine. The smoke cleared. The Protector saw the familiar form of the Robot toss a man into two other men. A few paces away, the Understudy cracked a brawler's gun hand with her baton.

The cavalry arriving in the nick of time was too much for Dufresne. He waved his remaining men back. They dashed for the warehouse door, pinning the trio under a hail of covering fire. The Robot shielded the Protector and the Understudy.

Once the gangsters were through the door, the Robot rushed after them.

"Never mind!" The Protector said. "Let them go."

The Robot halted.

"How'd you find me?" the Protector asked the Understudy.

"An informant."

"One of Dufresne's men," the Robot said. "She …encouraged his cooperation."

"He was very cooperative."

The Protector glanced to the Robot and back at the Understudy.

"I have the feeling there is more to this than you're telling me."

"No. Oh wait, Yes. One small detail." The Understudy grinned. "There was a chainsaw involved."

"Tell me more later—or maybe don't tell me at all, kid."

The Robot surveyed the incapacitated men on the floor.

"You allowed them to capture you," the Robot said. "You could have escaped at any time."

"Almost any time," the Protector admitted. "There were a few moments when I really was at their mercy."

"But they never knew," said the Understudy.

"Of course." The Protector gazed around the warehouse. He let out a brief exclamation and picked up his bunched coat from the floor. He inspected the contents of the pockets as he continued speaking, "I poked around his rail yard until I got caught. I wanted to talk with him."

"Why did you want to talk—get caught—whatever?" asked the Understudy

"I was trying the age-proven tactic of divide and conquer." The Protector shrugged on his coat. "I was hoping to put Medina and Dufresne at each other's throat."

The Protector glanced around, searching.

"We've got your hat."

"Oh, good."

"So, you're still investigating the murder of the Alien, after all."

"He was a friend. Regardless of the weapon used," the Protector eyed the Robot critically. "Medina gave the order to pull the trigger. I'm sure of it."

If the Robot noticed the Protector's assessing gaze, it gave no indication.

"Is your plan progressing?" the Robot asked.

"Yes. They're divided, but I still need to step in and conquer. That's why I called you off. I want Dufresne free. I think he's sorer with Medina than with me—for now." The Protector turned his attention to the Understudy. "What are you doing here?"

"Why does everyone keep wondering why I'm where I am?" the Understudy asked. "Look—never mind. The Robot is innocent. You can take my word for it now. And if not, I don't know what else to say. I saw Medina's proxy, Josephine…she tried to kill him—a few times."

The Protector look squarely at the Robot, his expression softened.

"I'm glad of that. I truly am."

"Great," the Understudy grabbed each of their right hands. She couldn't budge the Robot, but she pulled the Protector forward. "Shake. We're all a happy family again."

The man and the machine shook hands.

"What now?" the Robot asked.

"We get back to Pallas. It could be a real gangland bloodbath," the Protector said. "Well, Medina doesn't have a gang, but he's got enough martial tech to put a big hole in Dufresne's guys."

"Should we just let them? I mean, they are the bad guys," the Understudy said.

"Police will get called. Emergency services. We don't want innocent people in the crossfire."

"It would also be a good distraction," the Robot said. "We can, perhaps, get inside the factory while Medina's attention is elsewhere."

"I like the way you think," said the Protector.

Once again, as on the night the Alien had been assassinated, the Understudy hid at the edge of the property where Medina's factory stood. The tall pines kept them in shadow. The Protector and the Robot flanked her. They were on the lookout for Dufresne and his crew, but no one had arrived.

The mobster and his team had slipped into Pallas early in the morning, having driven straight from Crowsport overnight. They had come in ones and twos and spread out across hotels in the city, trying not to alert Medina to their presence.

The Protector had predicted a night raid.

"I'm surprised we beat them here," the Understudy said. They'd been waiting in the dark for hours.

"You shouldn't be. They had to stop and suit up for war. We had the Robot's flying car." The Protector scanned the area with binoculars. The Robot's hover-car had landed at the opposite end of the copse. "Nice automobile, by the way. We should find a way to make it invisible."

"Why?" asked the Robot.

"Why not?" The Protector shrugged. "It'll be a challenge. I wonder if the Alien left an invisibility circuit lying around. It should be an easy adaptation. It sounds like something he'd have left lying around. Or maybe a chameleon circuit."

"I bet there were a lot of things the Alien could have done, given time." The Understudy felt a touch of melancholy.

"Speaking of alien tech gadgets—did you ever find any secret projects the Alien worked on before he created you?" the Protector asked. "You've always been online since your inception, so if there's anything you didn't know about him it would have been before then."

"What kind of gadget are you thinking of?" asked the Understudy.

"The Alien knew how powerful he was. If he ever went rogue, nothing could stop him. Unless he planned for it."

"You are suggesting the Alien might have created the weapon used to assassinate him?" the Robot asked. "I have not found any such record. I can research this idea, but the Lair has been heavily damaged. If there were records, they could be lost forever."

"It was a long shot. I'm still trying to figure out how Medina did it. How did he kill the Alien?" The Protector shook his head. "How do you reduce a super-being to a pile of ash, short of dropping an atomic bomb on him?"

The factory showed more signs of productivity than it had the night the Alien died. The lights were on. There was a murmur of industry behind the walls. The most significant change was the presence of armed guards. They were panning spotlights around the property and patrolling the grounds.

"Why do you think this factory has something of more value than any of Medina's other factories?" the Robot asked.

"Deception and validation," the Understudy answered before the Protector could. "Before, there was no special security, no night shift workers. But there was that centaur-bot. A big investment to leave standing around an ordinary manufacturing plant."

"And now," the Protector pointed at the strolling guards, "No more facade. Straight up heightened security."

The Understudy saw a line of headlights moving along the road.

"Here they come."

Four black limousines and two large black SUVs drove up the entrance road. They fanned out off the road in a semicircle. The lead limousine stopped with its nose inches from the main gate.

Medina's guards were wary. Guns were readied. The driver stayed in the vehicle; four men climbed out. They were all large and well built, their suits cut to show strong physiques. Dufresne came out last. The four bodyguards surrounded him as he walked to the gate.

Medina's men turned the spotlights on the cars and gangsters. A cluster of guards approached the gangsters at the gate. Dufresne addressed the lead facility guard.

"What are they saying?" the Protector asked the Robot.

The Robot stared at the men. The Understudy wondered if the Robot could read lips. More likely, the curved indents along the sides of its head served as parabolic dishes as well as simple ears.

"Dufresne is demanding an audience with Medina."

"What's their answer?"

Gunfire. Pistols popped and submachine guns chattered. Muzzles flashed yellow-orange in the dark.

Two of Dufresne's bodyguards fell. The mob boss and his two remaining bodyguards took cover behind open car doors. They returned fire with their comrades, and three of Medina's guards went down. Two were saved by the bulletproof vests they wore, but the force of the slugs incapacitated them. The third guard had a leg wound.

A siren blared. Warning lights of yellow and white flashed in the night. With a clanging thud, the large hatch in the center of the grounds flipped open.

"Here it comes," the Protector said.

The giant centaur-bot sprouted from the ground like a mechanical tree. Its head rotated, surveying the situation.

"Hostile elements attempting to penetrate interior." Legs pumping, the centaur-bot loped toward the gate. "Destroy."

Cable tentacles shot out from its arm and wove their way through the chain link fence. The centaur-bot pulled. A portion of the fence tore away, leaving ragged, twisted wire in its wake. The centaur-bot leapt through the gap.

Dufresne's men had engaged in heavy firefights with other criminal gangs before, but fighting a machine monster was something else entirely. They hesitated, unsure whether to attack or retreat.

"Shut your gaping jaws and shoot!" Dufresne yelled. The

mob boss drew his own pistol—an old oversized revolver—and shot at the robotic monstrosity.

The mobsters opened fire on the centaur-bot towering over them. Slugs dented the metal but failed to penetrate. One mechanical foot stomped down on the hood of a limousine, while a tendril tore away the door and grabbed the two men sheltering there. The tentacles whipped and the men went sailing through the air, hitting the ground many yards away. The robot attacked the next vehicle in line.

"I think now would be a good time to get inside that factory," the Protector said.

"I thought we were here to protect the innocent."

"They haven't shown up yet. Just the mobsters."

"We should protect them," the Robot said. "Even if they are criminals."

"This is our best chance," the Protector said. "They'll need to fend for themselves."

The Understudy didn't argue. She felt the same pull on her curiosity. What was coming off the assembly line inside? What required a giant centaur-bot and other heavy defenses?

Something exploded under the centaur-bot's chin. The Understudy saw one of Dufresne's men come out of a crouch, toss away a spent rocket launcher. Part of the bot's head was mangled. Sparks spit and fluid leaked.

"More rockets?" said the Understudy.

"I think Dufresne was skimming off the top," said the Protector. "There's only one source for those rocket launchers."

"Medina," said the Robot.

"Fight fire with fire," the Understudy said. "Poetic. I like it."

Another flash. A smoke trail tracked through the gap in the fence. It impacted the ground near a cluster of Medina's guards and tossed them into the air.

"No better moment."

The Understudy broke from cover. She tried her best to stay unnoticed as she approached the fence from what she hoped was an oblique angle. The Protector and the Robot ran with her.

Dufresne's men were turning the tide of the battle. Another rocket exploded in the underbelly of the centaur-bot as it tore apart a second car. One of its legs separated and fell away. It stumbled, but regained footing on three legs after a few shaky moments.

At the corner of the fence, the Understudy crouched. The Robot and Protector came up beside her. She looked down the length of the barrier to the spot where the firefight lit up the night.

She glanced up. If they were spotted half-way through their climb—a coincidental glance in their direction would be enough—both the guards and Dufresne's goons would shoot them down.

"We're going to need a lift," the Protector said.

Before the Understudy could protest, the Robot grabbed her jacket in one hand and the Protector's coat in the other. The Robot flew upward. Just when the cinch of her jacket reached an uncomfortable threshold, her feet touched the ground inside the fence.

"A pair of wings would be ridiculously unwieldy," the Protector straightened his long coat and hat, "but I could adapt your anti-grav tech into some sort of belt unit. That would be useful."

"If humans were meant to fly…." the Understudy said.

The Protector forestalled her with a raised hand.

They ran to the side of the building and inched around the corner. The men fighting on the grounds had not spotted them. The trio sheltered in the front doorway of the building.

"We still need to penetrate the factory." The Robot examined the keypad entry. "Medina's security is difficult to breach. It will take too much time."

"We just need to wait," the Protector said. "I expect an opportunity sooner rather than later, considering how the fight is going."

The Understudy turned her attention to the battle. She understood what the Protector meant. The giant centaur-bot had fallen on its side. One of the gangsters had jumped into the driver seat of one of the limousines. The vehicle spun tires in reverse and then shot forward, ramming the centaur-bot. The other mobsters had taken down all of Medina's guards.

They were stepping through the gate, headed toward the main entrance. Dufresne directed from the rear, his one remaining bodyguard still at his side.

Beside the doorway entrance, there was a garage door, windowless and composed of metal slats. The bottom was flush with the ground.

The door started to rise.

"Another giant robot?" the Understudy said.

"I'm going to guess standard reinforcements—and our chance," said the Protector.

The Protector had guessed correctly: guards emerged, more heavily armed and armored than their counterparts. They advanced under covering fire. An armored personnel carrier rolled out behind them.

The Understudy wondered what had taken them so long to join the fray. Then she recalled how time seemed to slow when she was fighting. It felt like hours, but only a few minutes had passed. The guards outside had delayed Dufresne's attack while personnel in the factory had readied to deploy.

"This factory must be important to Medina to fight so hard for it," the Robot said. "Otherwise, he might have scuttled the place when the fight had first turned, as he did with the train."

The Protector nodded in agreement.

The guards advanced, focused on the battle. The garage door was descending. The trio ran, ducking inside before anyone noticed them.

They stood in an open cargo space: gray, bare, and utilitarian. A freight elevator occupied the far end. It was quiet inside the factory, as though the entire staff had been mustered to deal with Dufresne's attack.

"Let's see where they came from," the Protector said.

The trio stepped into the elevator. The Understudy was relieved to see the controls were simple. There were no keys or keypad security. She didn't want any moments wasted. Someone was going to win the battle outside, but the outcome didn't matter. Both sides were hostile.

The elevator descended toward the expansive factory floor, deep underground. Through the open grating of the elevator walls, multiple assembly lines could be seen. Finished products stood lining the walls. There were hundreds of them.

The Understudy let out a gasp.

"They look familiar," the Robot said.

"Was that humor?" asked the Understudy.

"It was a statement of fact."

As far as their eyes could see, a robot army stood at attention, while more of their ilk stepped away from the end of the assembly conveyors and marched to join the others. Except for their white outer shells, binary eyes, and forest green highlights, each was a carbon copy of the Robot.

The trio stepped out onto the factory floor. The Understudy fought to keep fear from overrunning her imagination. The machines were dormant, but if the entire legion of robots came online, she didn't like their chances of getting out of the factory.

"So. You have thrown all legal pretense to the wind and simply broken into my property. With what purpose? Sabotage?"

Milton Medina stepped out from the ranks of robots, his bald head glistening under the lights. He wore a black suit tailored to his muscular frame. He carried no weapons, but something in his gaze led the Understudy to imagine the man was a weapon. He walked with surety and smoothness. If he was anything less than a black belt in some form of martial arts, she would be surprised.

"I think we have a copyright suit on our hands," the Protector said. "Your design isn't exactly original."

The Robot walked along the closest rank of the white robots, leaning in close, seeming to study the automatons. If they were automatons. The Understudy wondered if they had internal programming to match the Robot.

"I know you have not had access to the Alien's files," the Robot said. "These machines might look like me, but I am certain their internals are primitive by my standards. No offense meant."

"None taken. I didn't need the Alien's files. I went to the source."

Medina stepped aside. With a flourish he turned sideways and held an arm out behind him.

From the rear of the large room, another robot was gliding toward them, hovering above the floor. It came to a stop beside Medina and settled to the floor.

Before them was a mirror opposite of the Robot, its body red with black highlights. Its single red eye, an exact match for that of the Robot, glared as in a baleful menace. Its metal casing was not pristine, however. There were dents and scorch marks. If the material used in its construction was the same as the Robot's, the Understudy dreaded to think what the Red Robot had encountered to create the scars on its body.

The Red Robot turned from the Protector to the Understudy and then to the Robot. The Understudy did not like being under the gaze of that eye.

"You must be a prototype." the Protector said. He pointed at the Robot. "A model the Alien created before this one."

"No. Not at all." The Red Robot's voice was a match for the Robot's. It held out its right arm toward the Robot. "That is the inferior copy. I am the original. The Alien did not create me. His people did."

"They sent you here to kill the Alien?"

The Red Robot titled its head.

"No. I came here with the Alien. We were on a mission."

"Why have you thrown in with Medina?" The Protector asked. "What do you intend to do?"

"I intend to carry out the mission. The mission Vythor—the Alien—betrayed."

"So, his name was Vythor. Interesting," the Protector said. "What is your mission?"

"The mission was to scout this planet. Now the charter and parameters of that mission have changed."

"You have a new mission," the Understudy said. "What is it?"

"My mission is to conquer humanity and claim this world for the Haephotian Empire," the Red Robot said.

11. AN ARMY ON THE MARCH

The silence was unnerving. The Red Robot's pronouncement hung in the air. In face of the alien machine, the Understudy felt a cold menace. Ranks of immobile robots lined the factory floor as far as her eye could see.

Medina scowled, hot with anger. He turned to the Red Robot.

"What are you talking about? This army is earmarked for an African military coup."

The Protector laughed.

"What's so funny?" Medina snarled.

"You didn't dig deep enough. Isn't it obvious? The Red Robot here is your African client."

"The Protector's deduction is correct," said the Red Robot.

"Who's the power behind the throne, Medina? You didn't think you were the grand orchestrator, did you?" The Protector shook his head. "You're smart, Medina. But money and vanity make you stupid. There isn't a junta in Africa with enough money to pay for this tech. The only African country which could afford this doesn't need it. And they don't deal with outsiders. You didn't do your homework."

"I did check!" Medina snarled. "I triple-checked!"

"You should have checked a few more times." The Protector pointed at the Red Robot. "You know how good robots are at digital infiltration. Apparently, this one is good at manipulation, too. Then again, your personality makes it easy."

"It is time," the Red Robot said.

The army of robots came to life. Eyes lit red. Arms and legs twitched as power surged through their mechanical bodies.

Their heads turned as one to the left, observing their red leader. They were as coordinated as soldiers on parade—even more so, being programmed machines of logic.

"Oh no you don't!"

Medina pulled a white, handheld device from the pocket of his suit coat. Gloating, he lifted it over his head and pressed the button.

Nothing happened.

Confusion etched the magnate's face. He clicked the button again, and again, until he squeezed his thumb white. His face was a red sheet of anger.

"I am aware of the self-destruct protocols in all your military products," the Red Robot said. "I have overridden them."

Medina dropped the device, face scrunched in a moue of disbelief. He took shaky steps away from the Red Robot until he stood beside the Robot and the other two humans.

"You can take some comfort in this robotic conquest of humanity, Medina." The Protector sounded unperturbed. He might as well have been confronting a clumsy, first-time mugger rather than a robot army bent on subjugating humanity. "You'll be first to die along with us."

"Way to go, Milton," the Understudy said. "Killed by your own soldier-bots."

The army stepped forward in unison. Their metallic feet stomped like a peal of thunder. They shifted their bodies, faced the freight elevator.

"Sweep them aside," the Red Robot said.

Another clanking crash of thunder.

And another.

The three humans backed away. The Robot remained, studying its red predecessor.

"Suggestions?" asked the Protector.

"Stairs? There must be stairs in case of fire."

"Other side of the floor—through them." Medina pointed at the ranks of soldier-bots.

"Elevator it is, then," the Protector said.

They continued their retreat.

"Come on, Robot!" The Understudy waved the Robot to join them.

The Robot stepped back but did not take its gaze from the Red Robot.

The soldier-bots plodded forward. If they weren't logical machines, the Understudy would have thought they were toying with them.

"Did you program them to be cats who like to play with mice?" the Understudy asked Medina.

"They're warming up," Medina said. "They'll come after us soon."

"Smoke screen?" said the Understudy.

"If they have sensor systems like mine, smoke will do little to confound them," the Robot said.

"My smoke will work," the Protector said. "I've adapted it with interfering ores. But they'll still hear us."

"Sonic disruption along with the smoke." Medina had gotten over his shock. He bristled. He rattled off a frequency. "Bursts would be more disruptive than a single signal, if we could manage it."

The Protector pulled a thick pen from the lapel pocket of this long coat. He handed it to the Understudy. The pen wasn't a pen. The device had two controls: a toothed-gear dial, and a button.

"I'm not sure the frequency will be high enough. I had trouble getting it above dogs and into the Alien's range." The Protector pointed to a dial in the shaft. The Understudy spun the disc to its far range. "It's not designed to burst. You need to press it, every three seconds."

The Understudy nodded.

"Now!" yelled Medina.

The Understudy pressed the button. The soldier-bots halted mid-step. They lost their synchronicity. Some continued to step, others did not. One spun in confusion, bumping into its close-ranked brethren. A wave of stumbling and discoordination swept through the mechanical platoon.

The Protector threw smoke capsules. They flashed on the floor, enveloping the humans and the Robot. They ran for the elevator. The Understudy wondered how fast the soldier-bots could run. Could they even hope to get the elevator in motion before the machines covered the distance?

The Protector cussed as they emerged from the smoke cloud.

The Red Robot waited at the doors. It had flown over the smoke cloud, knowing the elevator was their only egress from the factory floor.

"Go!" the Robot commanded.

The Robot flew at the Red Robot. The two machines grappled in mid-air. Behind, the Understudy heard the even tread of marching machines. The robot army had recovered from the sonic attack. The smoke was dissipating. She pressed the button on the device again. The soldier-bots continued their march.

Medina saw her frustration.

"They've stopped scanning the frequency range."

She jammed the sonic pen into her pocket.

The Protector pulled the freight elevator doors open.

"Come on!"

Medina didn't hesitate. He ran into the elevator.

The Understudy ran but halted at the threshold. In the air, the Red Robot and the Robot threw punches, parried, swooped, and dived. Each blow sounded like a hammer against an anvil. She wondered how much abuse they could take from each other.

The smoke cleared. The blue-green army of soldier-bots had halted. Perhaps they were considering whether to continue after the humans or aid their leader.

The Protector pulled the Understudy inside the elevator. The doors slammed shut. The elevator started to rise.

"No! We need to help the Robot!"

"We're outclassed." The Protector sounded tired. He must be if he'd allow even a hint of fatigue or weakness to show in front of her—or Medina—or anyone. "We need to regroup. Until then...."

The Understudy slumped her shoulders.

"The Robot fights alone."

The Robot pushed upward. The Red Robot matched its strength and shoved down. Beneath them, the soldier-bots tilted their heads to watch the battle. They did not appear to have any weapons built into their systems, or they would have fired at the Robot. Their armory must have been located at another of Medina's factories.

The Red Robot fired the maneuvering thruster in its left sole. The Robot had not expected the imbalanced pressure. They spiraled into the wall with an impact that cracked the concrete. The Robot's right hand lost its grip. The Red Robot smashed a fist at the Robot's eye. The Robot punched at the Red Robot's abdomen. The Red Robot responded with a blur of punches at the Robot's torso. A structural integrity warning flashed through the Robot's awareness. A hairline fracture had cracked across its chest.

The Robot protected its chest. Another pummeling would increase the damage. The Red Robot redoubled its efforts to hit the weakened area. The Robot ran scans, detected no appreciable damage on its opponent.

The Red Robot glanced down at the soldier-bots below. It turned its head upward and saw the freight elevator rising.

"Continue as ordered." The Red Robot swiveled its head to gaze eye-to-eye with the Robot. "This is a temporary distraction."

The soldier-bots turned their attention away from the aerial battle and marched forward. They halted at the doors awaiting the elevator's return.

The Robot grabbed the Red Robot's hand and tried to push out from the wall. The Red Robot countered, keeping the Robot pinned.

"We are at a standstill," the Robot said.

"You have been damaged. I am the superior construct," the Red Robot said. "Your mirroring of my design is only external. You are the cobbled together patchwork of a criminal. You will yield."

"Perhaps eventually. But you have a plan in execution. How much delay can you afford?"

The Red Robot spun, pulling the Robot out from the wall, and threw the Robot downward.

The soldier-bot ranks below parted as the Robot smashed

into the floor, its body resting in a crater of concrete rubble. Something cracked. Its sensors momentarily jumbled, the Robot did not know which part of its body had been compromised.

The soldier-bots surged forward. The Robot punched, sent one soldier-bot careening into its comrades. They fell over like bowling pins.

Many hands grappled the Robot's arms and legs. Anti-gravity drive engaged and foot boosters flaring, it could not pull free. No individual soldier-bot was a match for the Robot's strength, but in unison they were strong enough to restrain the Robot.

The Red Robot descended to the ground. Its feet clanged on the floor. It looked at the Robot and nodded, as if in satisfaction of the Robot's predicament.

"Squad Eight. Squad Nine." The Red Robot's voice gave no indication of any distress concerning the physical struggle in which it had engaged. It was not human. It did not have muscles to fatigue, or breath to catch. "Use the stairs. Destroy those humans and any more you find outside."

Two of the rear ranks of the soldier-bots turned on their heels and marched toward the opposite end of the factory floor.

The Understudy bit her lip. She was concerned for the Robot, fighting the Red Robot somewhere below. The freight elevator rose out of the underground facility. They could still hear the metallic thunder of battle. She wished Medina had stolen tech from the Alien's penthouse elevator. They ascended too slow.

"Suggestions?" Medina asked.

"I was going to ask you the same," the Protector said.

"Let's get back to the hover-car." The Understudy looked at Medina. "It's southeast on the other side of the woods."

"That's our rendezvous point if we get separated," the Protector said.

"Then what?" asked the magnate.

"We get into the air. Then we figure what to do next," the Protector said.

The Understudy didn't find much comfort in the ad hoc plan. Gangsters were one thing; the Red Robot had an army and a plan. They needed a counterplan.

"Why don't we figure out what the Red Robot is going to do next?"

"The armory," Medina replied. "Those robots don't have any built-in weapons."

"Fine." The Protector nodded. "We'll go there."

"And head them off." Medina slapped his fist into his palm. His eye lit with a grim satisfaction.

"No, we destroy it."

Medina's lips tightened. The two men glared at one another. The Understudy attempted to defuse the confrontation.

"We're almost at the top," she noted.

The men continued their staring contest.

"It will be easier to destroy the place than to fight off an army," the Protector said.

Medina broke off his glare.

"Fine."

Medina, either overconfident in the ability of his new security arrangements, or distracted by the Red Robot's betrayal, yanked open the doors of the elevator. The Protector missed grabbing Medina's arm, and the Understudy's warning cry fell silent before it started.

Dufresne and his surviving men were waiting. They were haggard, wounded, and angry. They trained their guns on the trio in the elevator.

The Protector held his palm outward.

"Hold your fire!"

"Gimme a reason why I should?"

Taking advantage of Dufresne's momentary hesitation, the Protector ushered Medina and the Understudy out of the elevator.

"We're all you've got." The Protector stepped out and pulled the freight doors shut. The elevator immediately began its descent.

"For what?"

"There's a robot army under our feet, right now," the Understudy said. "They'll be here when the elevator gets back."

Dufresne's gorilla-sized bodyguard jabbed a thumb over his

shoulder. Out in the field, the Understudy saw the sparking, smoking remains of the centaur-bot. It struggled to move, but it only had one leg remaining. Its cable tentacles lashed futilely.

"His robots ain't so tough," the goon said.

"That's only one," the Protector said. "A large and difficult one to take down, certainly. But I don't think there are enough of us left to tackle a bunch of robot soldiers."

"Maybe we should just kill their leader, then." Dufresne pointed his pistol at Medina.

"He's not their leader; the Red Robot is," the Understudy said.

"The what?" Dufresne scowled in ignorance.

"Look," the Protector eyed the elevator doors warily, "Long story, we don't have time. We need Medina alive. We all need each other alive right now."

The Understudy heard soldier-bots marching. It was the unmistakable metallic clanking she'd heard on the factory floor below, except the ground muffled the sound a bit. The others looked around, too, attempting to locate the source.

The Understudy shot a perplexed look at the freight doors. "How?"

"They took the stairs!" the Protector said.

The pairs of red eyes appeared from around the corner of the building. The blue-green metallic bodies seemed to glow under the outside lights of the facility. It wasn't the entire army they'd seen below, but there were more than enough soldier-bots to overwhelm them. They had no means of stopping the machines. Dufresne's gang might have more rocket launchers on hand, but more likely, they'd fired all they had to take down the centaur-bot.

"Run!" the Protector shouted.

No one disputed the command.

The Robot strained to pull its limbs free, but the soldier-bots did not yield their hold. It was a stalemate. There were no biological muscles in play. The Robot's strength did not fatigue. Neither did that of its captors.

The elevator had returned and stood open and waiting.

There seemed to be no urgency. The soldier-bots not holding the
Robot remained stationary. The dispatched portion of the army
was capable enough to stop the current threat. That might be an
advantage. The Red Robot did not understand how resourceful
the Protector and the Understudy could be—and Medina, as
well.

The Red Robot studied its captive.

"Why do you hesitate?" the Robot asked. "Shouldn't you
destroy me—order your soldier-bots to pull me apart?"

"I am evaluating the damage to your systems." The Red
Robot circled the cluster of soldier-bots holding the Robot.
"You are not equal to my specifications. But you are far more
advanced than these machines. With reprogramming, you
might prove useful."

The Robot had never considered its individuality. It was
a robot, a machine, built to perform its function and that was
what it did. It had a desire not to become a tool of the Red
Robot. Its programming for justice and law contributed to its
resistance. But there was something more. In a way it could not
analyze or comprehend, the Robot had something extra in its
programming. Perhaps the Alien had experimented with an
artificial psyche.

Perhaps it had not been an experiment. Perhaps it was a gift.

The Robot existed. The Robot was sentient.

The Robot would not allow the Red Robot to erase everything
it had become.

The Understudy, the Protector, and Medina fled into the darkness
of the pines. Dufresne and his remaining men followed. The
beat of the soldier-bots' stomping feet came steadily after them.
They could outrun the machines. In the long term, though, they
would tire. The soldier-bots would not.

The Protector glanced over his shoulder, held up a hand.
They paused for breath.

"Can't we shut them down somehow?" the Understudy
asked.

"The Red Robot disabled the self-destruct."

"No, the Red Robot overrode the code. It's still active,"

Medina said. "The circuit can't be removed. Its redundancy failsafe would initiate the self-destruct."

"Can you override the override?" asked the Protector.

"Get me into my network, somehow, and maybe I can," Medina said.

"I suspect you'll find what you need in the hover-car."

"Then let's keep moving," Medina said.

They started off again just as Dufresne and his men arrived. One of the goons groaned. They'd missed their chance to rest. They pushed on, following the trio.

The Understudy felt relieved when she spotted the hover-car. They broke from the tree line and ran toward the futuristic vehicle.

"Hold it!" Dufresne shouted from behind them. "Nobody gets in that car without my say-so."

The trio halted and turned around. The mobsters were exhausted but not out of the fight. They had their guns aimed at the trio.

"Oh, for cryin' out loud!" The Protector threw his arms up, in exasperation rather than surrender. "Now isn't the time."

"Nobody's driving off without us," the big goon said.

"Without me, you mean," Dufresne said.

"Sure, boss, sure." The goon frowned at his own capitulation.

"Doesn't matter," the Understudy said.

"What doesn't matter?" Dufresne said.

She knocked on the plexiglass dome of the hover-car.

"Locked. We don't have the key."

"Well, who does?" Dufresne demanded.

The Protector sighed.

"The Robot."

Pinned down, the Robot redoubled its efforts to break free. The result was negligible—a slight shift here, the whine of a servo under more stress there. The effort was futile and would remain so unless the Robot could find some new angle of leverage.

The Red Robot silently continued to appraise its prisoner. Finally, it nodded, as a human would when a decision had been reached.

"No. No, I do not think I will," the Red Robot said. "Detaining you until I have the opportunity to wipe your programming will take too much time."

The Robot considered the statement. There was a factory full of soldier-bots at the Red Robot's disposal. For all the Robot and its allies knew, the Red Robot had set up more factories, perhaps through other tech companies. One legion of mechanical troops was not enough to conquer humanity in a drawn-out war. Perhaps the Red Robot hoped to make a decisive first strike with the soldier-bots at hand.

Or there must have been another reason.

"Your plan is time critical," the Robot said.

The Red Robot did not react. The Robot inferred it had—as humans might say—struck a nerve.

"Tear this machine apart," the Red Robot ordered. "The rest of you, come with me."

The Red Robot floated away without a backward glance.

The army marched in its wake.

The remaining soldier-bots lifted the Robot and held it parallel to the ground. They pulled on the Robot's leg, arms, and head. The Robot felt its servos grinding, increasing counter pressure.

It would take time, but the soldier-bots would eventually pull the Robot apart.

One of Dufresne's men smashed at the dome with the butt of his pistol. He grunted in pain as the shock traveled up his arm.

"That won't work." The Protector searched the pockets of his long coat.

"Better think of something quick," Medina said. "Or we might as well keep running."

The Protector held up his forefinger in reply. His other hand continued its rummage.

"Ah." The Protector triumphantly showed a whistle.

"This isn't London," the Understudy said. "No bobbies are going to come running."

The Protector blew into the whistle. There was no sound.

He gave another blow. Again, nothing happened. He rolled his eyes. He blew a third time.

The hover-car's interior lights glowed to readiness as the dome slid away.

"Dog whistle," the Protector said, returning the item to his coat—in a pocket which was not the one from which he had pulled it. "The Robot's key is a high frequency sound."

"Enough prattle!" Medina leapt into the passenger seat, ignoring Dufresne's earlier threats. He studied the layout of the cockpit.

The Protector reached in, flipped a lever. A holographic keyboard displayed under Medina's fingertips.

"You know what to do," the Protector said to Medina. He turned to Dufresne. "Medina will try to shut down those soldier-bots. That won't stop the Red Robot. Maybe we're not important enough to bother with anymore. I don't know. We need to cover Medina until he's finished."

The crime boss wasn't pleased, but he accepted the situation.

"What do you recommend?"

"If your boys are good shots, aim for the joints—the knees especially, but elbows, too. Those are going to be the weakest points—maybe the only weak points."

"All right." Dufresne waved a hand at his remaining men. "Get behind some trees."

The gangster spoke to the Protector. "What are you gonna do? Stand around while we do all the work?"

"I'm going to try setting a trap." The Protector said. "So kindly get in position. I wouldn't want you to get killed—yet."

Dufresne glared and huffed, then he joined his men.

In the distance, the sound of the soldier-bots had paused. The Understudy didn't like the silence, it harbored more foreboding than pleasantness.

"Why have they halted?" she asked.

The Protector stared ahead into the darkness as if he could see through the woods.

"Awaiting a change of orders, maybe." The Protector turned to Medina. "Are you in yet?"

"Almost. The Alien got rather farther in than I'd imagined."

The Protector chuckled.

"I'll bet that was the Robot's doing more than the Alien's."

"Really?" Medina scowled. "Remind me to sue him after this. You, too."

The Protector grabbed the Understudy's the elbow. "We should let him work in peace; I suppose."

They'd taken ten steps away when the thunder of the marching robot army renewed.

"Why does it sound louder? Tell me it's because they're closer, and not because there are more of them," the Understudy said.

"There are more of them," the Protector said.

"That's not what I told you to tell me."

The Protector shrugged.

"It sounds like the entire army just mobilized. I guess the squad chasing us is waiting for them to catch up."

"You had an idea for a trap," the Understudy said.

"I thought to tap the power of the hover-car to run hot wire across some trees," the Protector said.

"But?"

"We don't have a long enough length of wire." The Protector pulled a coil of thin wire from his pocket. "All I've got. Not sure it could handle the charge, anyway." He slipped the wire back into his pocket. "And we can't risk a power drain undermining Medina's work."

The Understudy saw red eyes and the glint of colored metal coming through the trees. She wanted to scream at the soldier-bots' relentless methodical march. She almost wished the machines had guns and would start shooting—act human in some way. She wondered why the machines elicited such a reaction in her psyche. She had been enjoying the Robot's company. Perhaps that was the cause. The soldier-bots were hollow, lifeless automatons compared to the Robot.

"Probably no time now, anyway," she said.

"No, I think not," the Protector said.

"We're missing something here," the Understudy said.

"What?"

"That's a big army, but it's a drop in the bucket against

humanity. Even if they are all as strong as the Robot, heavy weapons could probably take them out."

"You noticed that, too." The Protector gave the Understudy an approving grin. "You're learning."

"So, this little army..."

"...is a means to an end," the Protector finished her statement. "But not the end itself."

The Robot felt its left elbow yielding to the force applied. Programmatic self-preservation engaged. It fought to save its arm. The mechanical joint continued to give way. Once the weak point developed, the result was inevitable. It would lose the bottom half of its arm.

It would also produce an opportunity.

The Robot halted the commands to the servos in its arm. The pressure fell off in a moment. The resistance null, the bottom portion of its left arm gave way. Metal ripped and screeched, wires and other fibrous conduits sparked and fizzed.

The two soldier-bots pulling the arm fell backward. The Robot slammed its half arm into the robot at its left side. The weight of three soldier-bots removed, the Robot engaged its antigravity unit. It tried to rise, to bring the soldier-bots off the floor into the air where they would have no leverage.

The Robot failed.

The combined weight and strength of the remaining soldier-bots kept the Robot captive. Its right hip verged on a fracture which would soon tear wide open.

Its neck felt a growing pressure, too.

The soldier-bots extrapolated their crude attempt at linear dismantling. They increased their efforts in three dimensions, twisting and pulling. Some of the Robot's servos burst at the change in attack. Its right leg fell to forty-three percent utilization. The Robot locked its head into position, could hear its own neck squealing in metallic protest at the forces applied.

In minutes, the Robot's body would be nothing more than a scrap heap.

There was a violent jerking against its left leg. Spasmodic and unsystematic—even in their twisting the soldier-bots were precise. The Robot looked down its body and saw one of the blue-green soldier-bots twitching uncontrollably. The blue-green machine lost its hold on the Robot's leg. Sparks flew out from its eye, which faded from red to black nothing.

The other soldier-bots were similarly affected. They spasmed, spun. Some lost their grip on the Robot. Those still holding the Robot twitched in self-destruction, causing more damage. Eyes and faces blew out in a shower of sparks and hissing electrical arcs.

The soldier-bots collapsed into a heap of mechanical refuse, burying the Robot under their weight.

The Red Robot hovered just off the ground. It led its blue-green robot army toward the humans and the hover-car.

Dufresne's gangsters kept up a consistent gunfire. They didn't have much ammunition left and were trying to make their shots count, but the mobsters failed to hit vital points on any of the soldier-bots.

When the soldier-bots drew near, the mobsters broke off and ran. They did not bother retreating to the hover-car, but disappeared into the woods, running across the line of soldier-bots before the flank caught them.

"Well, they weren't going to be much more help, anyway," commented the Protector.

The first soldier-bots stepped from the woods, ranks following behind. They poised like a robotic tidal wave, ready to dash down on them.

The Red Robot lifted its arm as if to signal a charge. Instead, it spun around quickly and looked at its troops.

The soldier-bots lost their cohesion. Legs jerked and twitched. Their bodies spasmed as if in the throes of an ague. Sparks and jagged bolts of electricity burst from their faces. Red eyes went dead. Some remained standing, silent statues. Many, unbalanced when their system failed, toppled over.

The Red Robot gazed ahead at them. The Understudy knew it was illogical—the Red Robot shouldn't have had any emotions, any more than the Robot did. But the Red Robot's single red eye glowed baleful in the darkness.

Nine soldier-bots stood behind the Red Robot, still operational.

"I was wrong." Medina scowled. "The Red Robot did manage to remove the self-destruct circuits from some of them."

"His own little cadre," the Understudy said.

"You are more resourceful than I anticipated," the Red Robot said. "You must be eliminated."

"In the car, now!"

The Protector leaped into the hover-car.

The Understudy's brief hesitation was costly.

The dome descended. She saw the Protector and Medina yelling at each other. The words were silent behind the plexiglass. The Protector tried to reach controls. Medina blocked him. They struggled against each other.

Medina had meant to shut them both out. He wouldn't risk opening the dome again.

She returned her attention to the Red Robot and his cadre.

The nine soldier-bots ran forward. Their plodding march was over.

They were faster than the Understudy ever expected.

12. IN THE NIGHT SKY

The Robot had not been aware it had gone offline. A quick check of its internal chronometer informed him that only a few seconds had passed. Most of the lost time had been spent rebooting and calculating damage. The Robot could not rest and heal. It carried its damage until it could make repairs—if they could be made. Without the aid of the Alien, the Robot wasn't certain.

The Robot pushed against the weight of the soldier-bot bodies. It wriggled, crawled, and pulled until it was free. It struggled to rise, its halved arm and crippled left hip confounded its efforts.

It reviewed its damage report.

The Robot's anti-gravity unit was still intact. It lifted from the floor and stood. It studied the jagged stump at its elbow. It could be repaired, but there was no time at the present. Taking a few steps, the Robot found it could walk—but not efficiently.

Flying it would be, then.

The Understudy had done a lot of running since she had started her crime-fighting tutelage with the Protector. They had chased perps, run in retreat, and dashed away before explosions killed them.

She had never run with such desperate speed and complete fear.

Two of the soldier-bots were on her tail. No glance over the shoulder was necessary. She knew they were getting closer. She heard their metal feet impact the ground with heavy thuds.

Her lungs burned. Her legs verged on cramping. It wasn't

fair. The machines didn't lose stamina. They didn't tire out.

Hard steel fingers pinched her shoulder. She had no breath to scream. She let out a whimper as she was hauled backward. She shifted. The cold fingers slipped off her shoulder but then grasped the bunched leather of her jacket.

The soldier-bot lifted her off the ground. Her feet flailed in the air.

The second soldier-bot came around and faced her. The blue green face and red eyes tilted as if examining her facial features.

The Understudy shivered under the cold, calculating, lifeless gaze.

The soldier-bot's hand reached for her face.

Something black and sleek streaked through the air, smashed into the soldier-bot's side. The soldier-bot crumpled to the ground. The black shape hovered where the soldier-bot had stood, turned to face the Understudy and her captor. It regarded them with its single red eye.

The Robot leapt forward. Its fist shot past the side of the Understudy's head and smashed into the soldier-bot's face. The punch crushed deep into the head, causing complete system failure. The soldier-bot's dormant fingers relaxed. The Understudy fell to the ground.

"Allow me."

The Robot reached for her with its left arm, which was half missing. Realizing its mistake, it offered her its right hand, instead.

The Understudy felt wobbly. The muscles in her legs protested. She fought through the aches and forced herself to inhale and exhale with some regularity.

"You are unhurt," There was a slight inflection at the end of the statement as though the Robot were asking her a question. She suspected it had performed a scan of her body.

"I think so." The Understudy couldn't see much in the dark. She wondered if there was more damage to the Robot than the missing half arm. "And you?"

"Functional." The Robot surveyed the damage it had done. The faceless soldier-bot was down, and the other lay on the ground some yards away. It wasn't moving. "I thought they had been shut down."

"Medina's doing. Yeah. Mostly, but not all of them." She grabbed the Robot's arm. "We need to help the Protector. He and Medina, they're in the hover-car. The Red Robot! The rest of the soldier-bots…."

In the distance, the interior light of the hover-car seeped out its clear dome. The light limned the robotic shapes with red eyes which attacked the vehicle. How much of the assault could the hover-car withstand?

"I saw. You were in the greater danger." The Robot rose a few inches off the ground. "I will attend to them. Stay h…." the Robot paused. "Follow when you are able."

The Robot streaked away.

"I think he knows me better than the Protector does," the Understudy muttered.

She tried to run toward the hover-car, but the agony in her chest and legs cut the effort short. She walked as fast as she could manage.

The soldier-bots swarmed over the vehicle. Like a scene from a zombie movie, their lifeless hands pawed at the dome. They threw their bodies against it. They tried to climb but slipped on the almost frictionless surface.

The Protector hardly noticed the danger outside. He was more concerned with keeping Medina from accessing the controls. The two men struggled, punching and grappling each other.

"Let me go, you fool," Medina shouted.

"Not a chance."

"You idiot—we could just drive away!"

"Not without my protégé."

"She's lost already."

That was a possibility the Protector did not want to hear. He'd always known the danger, preached about the danger, but in his heart, he never believed anything would happen to her. To him, sure. But the kid? No, that wouldn't be right.

But she was out there, beyond his help. Two soldier-bots were hunting her. Desperation and anger fueled a spike of adrenaline.

He let go of Medina's wrist. Before the magnate could react, the Protector's free fist clipped the side of his temple. Medina slumped forward, either unconscious or momentarily stunned.

The Protector engaged the forward control at full power. The headlights switched on automatically. The hover-car sped a few yards. He slammed on the brakes. The soldier-bots flew off the car, metallic fingers scratching as they lost their grips. As the soldier-bots recovered and stood, he ran the hover-car into their ranks. The crunching might have been robotic bodies or the body of the car—perhaps both. The Protector didn't know if he'd done enough to stop them, but it was all he could do.

He spun the hover-car in the direction he'd seen the Understudy run.

The headlights illuminated a robot in his path—a black robot with red highlights and a logo on its chest.

The Robot.

In the distance, coming along behind the Robot, the Protector saw a silhouette he would recognize anywhere. The Understudy was there. The soldier-bots that had chased her were nowhere to be seen.

The Protector sighed in relief.

The Robot was missing the bottom of its left arm, and sparks and tendrils of live power still fizzed at the stump. One leg seemed askew of the other. There were dents and scratches all over its body. The Robot lifted higher into the air, above the beams of the headlights. Against the dark sky, the Protector saw a hairline glow of energy across the Robot's chest. Its torso had been cracked.

The Robot flew over the hover-car, then swooped down, smashing into the remaining soldier-bots, using its already bashed body as a battering ram. The Protector wanted to ram the hover-car, but he couldn't maneuver the car without hitting the Robot, too.

The Protector leapt out of the hover-car and ran toward the Understudy.

A gunshot erupted like thunder; searing agony tore at his abdomen.

The Protector sprawled hard onto the ground.

The Understudy saw the glow of the Red Robot's eye, hovering over the pitched battle between its soldier-bots and the Robot. She saw the dome of the hover-car slide away, saw the Protector running to join her.

A small flash flared at the end of the Red Robot's extended arm.

The gunshot halted the Understudy in her tracks. She saw the Protector fall. She ran. The aching of her fatigued body went unnoticed. Her mind filled with dread. Her only goal was to reach the Protector's side. She did not even think to zigzag in case the Red Robot fired at her.

As she drew near to the Protector's still body, she glanced upward. The Red Robot had acquired a pistol—probably grabbed from a dead guard or mobster. It trained the weapon on her. She was too close to dodge. She closed her eyes.

Metal smashed against metal in a thunderous crush.

The Robot and the Red Robot grappled in the air.

Four of the soldier-bots had recovered from the Robot's assault.

The Understudy ignored their approach. She knelt beside the Protector. He was gasping in pain. She held his hand, felt hot tears streaming down her face. She heard the stamp of metal feet. She did not look away from her mentor.

"I am sorry," the Robot said.

She glanced up in surprise. The Red Robot was leading its remaining four soldier-bots into the dark of the trees.

"What?" She couldn't understand the Red Robot's departure.

"Tactical retreat." The Robot knelt beside her.

"They were beating us. They had us."

"But they do not have any more time." The Robot touched the Protector's chest. "What is his condition?"

"I don't know! He's not dead, but it looks bad."

"It is bad. The Red Robot shot to wound. If the Protector were dead, there would be no value in my remaining. This is a serious wound. I am obliged now to give aid. It will give the Red Robot time to escape."

"Let him go," the Understudy said. "We'll find him later."

"No!" The Protector grimaced and clutched at the Robot's arm. "This is far from over."

"Easy, easy," the Understudy said.

"The army is nothing." The Protector winced in pain with each word he forced out. "A distraction to keep Medina busy until the Red Robot was ready."

"Ready for what?"

"For...for...." The Protector's eyelids fluttered. His grip on the Robot relaxed. "Red ...Robot ...tried to kill Medina! Why? Why now?"

The Protector slipped into unconsciousness.

"No, no, no, no!" muttered the Understudy. "Stay with us! C'mon!"

The Protector's eyes snapped open.

"Elliptical orbit. Look...for...it." The words faded to a mumble, then he was quiet.

"No time for an ambulance." The Robot carried the Protector to the hover-car. It settled him into the passenger seat.

In the driver's seat, Medina moaned, started to come around. The Robot grabbed him by the suit coat, yanked him out, and dropped him unceremoniously. The magnate gazed around in a daze.

"Get in the driver seat," the Robot said to the Understudy.

She hopped in. The Robot's fingers blurred across the controls.

"I've programmed it to take you to the hospital. Stay with him. I must go after the Red Robot."

"No," the Understudy said. "Wait for me! You're damaged. You can't take on the Red Robot alone. Wait until we can regroup."

"There is no time."

"What are you talking about?"

"The robot army was a deception. It's not any part of the Red Robot's plan."

The dome of the hover-car descended.

"Where are you going?" The Understudy slapped at the dome.

The dome sealed shut and muffled her shouted protests.

The hover-car sped away, rising higher and higher into the air—the most direct route to the hospital.

The Robot lifted into the air, engaged the boosters in the soles of its feet, and disappeared into the night sky.

The Robot could have engaged the Red Robot and its remaining soldier-bots before they reached their destination. It could not be one hundred percent certain it had correctly deduced their intended destination, but it was the most probable.

The Robot was operating nowhere near peak efficiency.

It would need an advantage. It might need to sacrifice itself to stop the Red Robot. It had no hesitation making the sacrifice, but it needed to ensure such an action would include the destruction of the Red Robot, as well.

The Robot knew the Red Robot must be destroyed—foiling its plans would not be enough. The Red Robot would make other plans. The Red Robot was programmed to complete its mission. It would never stop.

The Robot alighted at the front entrance to the Moore-Rutledge observatory. The keypad entry had been upgraded since the break-in, but the improvement was not a hindrance. The Robot bypassed the security system and opened the door.

The Robot now understood who had broken in before. It suspected it knew the reason why they had used the telescope and removed all traces from the log.

There was time to learn if what it suspected were true. The lights stayed off. The Robot did not need them and did not want to alert the Red Robot to its presence. At the telescope controls, the Robot initiated the starting sequence. The dome roof retracted, exposing stars and the black night sky.

The Robot recalled the start and end coordinates which had bookended the missing section of the log. While the telescope could have been aimed anywhere, the Robot was confident, now, of what area to scan. It searched in an elliptical orbit, as the Protector had said.

Something glinted in view. The Robot narrowed the focus. On a display screen, the glint grew larger until it formed an odd image. It was blurred but not blurry, glinting but not reflecting light.

The Robot studied the spectral data. Some of the patterns seemed familiar. It took a few moments of memory scanning to recall. The Robot used the computer to enhance the image.

The image on the screen resolved.

A spaceship.

A spaceship in phase and out of phase with the space around it.

The spaceship was trapped in a subspace warp, orbiting through the solar system.

The Red Robot must have known. Must have always known. Why had it needed to break in and use the observatory telescope? The break-in had occurred weeks earlier. Why was time critical now?

A quick calculation of the spaceship's orbit gave the answer. The Robot could not say it knew. Only the Red Robot had the facts, but the Robot was confident it understood. It could hazard an accurate deduction.

Humanity was in far more danger than being at the mercy of a robot army.

The Red Robot arrived alone. Its remaining cadre of soldier-bots could not fly, and they could not march fast enough. The window of opportunity was closing. The physics could not be denied. The spaceship's orbit would soon pull it far away from Earth for years—perhaps decades. With an erratic and unknown quantity in the sub-warp, it was impossible to accurately predict when the spaceship might pass close again. The Red Robot needed to act; it had no other option.

The Robot had not bothered resetting the security systems. Their confrontation was inevitable. The Robot did not want civilians attracted to the battle zone.

The Red Robot floated into the rotunda.

The Robot was waiting.

"Why the army? Why the deception?" the Robot asked.

The Red Robot floated to the floor, stepped forward until it was face to face with the Robot. They tilted their heads in unison, cyclopean red eyes observing each other.

"It was not a deception, at first. I planned to create a robot army. Then I deduced what the Alien—Vythor—had become. Once I explained to Medina how the Alien could be killed, I needed to keep him distracted."

"You could have just assassinated Medina."

"I decided to keep the production of robots as a backup plan."

The Robot stepped over to the viewscreen. The spaceship blurred to watercolors, and then the image refocused.

"They are alive? How many?" the Robot asked.

"Two. Krev and Azomurn are their names," the Red Robot replied.

"Two with the power of the Alien—once they descend to Earth and absorb power from the sun."

"You never thought that was fact, did you?" The Red Robot seemed it would have laughed if it could. "Nonsensical. The solar radiation story was a fabrication. A deflection so no one would investigate Vythor's true source of power."

"But you did. You found his power and its weakness. Then you killed the Alien."

"Yes. I executed the traitor."

"How?"

"With a device of my own design."

"Medina has that device?"

The Red Robot shook its head. "There is no device now. It self-destructed when it destroyed the Alien. But Medina understands the principle. He is intelligent enough to build another one."

"That's why you wanted him distracted until you were ready. He could kill those two—Krev and Azomurn."

"Yes. Medina's usefulness is over. He cannot remain at large."

The patterns emerged as the Robot extrapolated data. Theories were formed and rejected. The scope of possibilities narrowed.

"The sub-warp!"

"You have determined the facts, at last. Yes. The exposure to the warp energies is what gave Vythor his superpower, not solar radiation."

"I recalled the spectral data from the penthouse the night of the assassination. I did not know it was sub-warp energy. I saw the spaceship exhibiting similar signatures tonight. The same strange energy signature. You created a warp device."

The Red Robot tilted its head slightly, as if nodding in response to a compliment.

"It overloaded Vythor's body; disintegrated him."

The Robot considered the new data. If it were human, it would have felt anger. It did not seek to avenge the Alien. It sought justice. Now it needed to protect humanity from an outside threat.

"Two more beings like the Alien," the Robot said. "Twice the power and potential of the Alien—at least. They have absorbed the radiation of the warp for years. They each might be more powerful than the Alien ever was."

"Yes. I calculate that, too." The Red Robot twisted its neck, focused on the image of the spaceship on the viewscreen. "They will subjugate this world in mere days. A week at the most."

"At Medina's factory, you stated they were on a scouting mission. They do not have the authority to commit conquest."

"I have the ability to improvise—as we have been programmed to do. Why waste the time and the resources to summon an invasion force? They will improvise, as well. They can conquer this planet swiftly and easily."

The Red Robot would have the moments calculated to the microsecond. The Robot wondered at its enemy's mental process—tried to guess algorithms of thought. Then the Robot realized the best way to think like the Red Robot was simply to think—they were undoubtedly programmed in similar manners.

"You are not hitching a ride on a rocket to intercept the craft. Radio communication would be difficult, if not impossible. And it might be discovered—even by accident." The Robot scanned the room, searching for something it had missed. "You are the one who stole Medina's laser. I conclude that is your planned method. You used this telescope before so that you could fine tune the variables of passing the laser through the sub-warp."

"Medina's laser, yes. With my enhancements it will contain

a coded signal. A signal which will disable the sabotaging device Vythor installed on the engine. The ship will break free of the sub-warp. Krev and Azomurn will again master their own destinies."

"I will stop you."

"You will be destroyed in the attempt."

"That possibility will not stop me."

The Robot lunged forward.

The Red Robot moved aside, smashing its fists down onto the Robot's back as it flew past.

The deflection sent the Robot smashing to the floor. The Red Robot swooped up near the top of the domed roof and then plummeted, its full weight smashing the Robot. The hairline crack in the Robot's chest threatened to crack wide open under the pressure of the impact. It held together, but the Robot calculated another blow would cause catastrophic damage.

The Red Robot knelt on the Robot's back, clutched the Robot's head on both sides. The Red Robot pulled, knee pushing down, bending the Robot's back. Mechanical vertebrae in the Robot's neck strained under the pressure. The Robot's right arm was pinned under its abdomen, its left stump flailed uselessly. It had no hand with which to grapple, no leverage to land a blow with any appreciable force.

The Robot fired the boosters in the sole of its left foot, spinning both robots around. The Red Robot's grip slipped. The Robot rolled and punched upward, knocking the Red Robot away.

The Red Robot hovered. The Robot tried to understand why it did not press the attack. The Red Robot was in midair. It was not protecting anything. It was not trying to reach anything. Time was wasting. The Red Robot would need to attempt to contact the ship soon.

The Robot recalled what the Alien had suggested. If someone had broken into the observatory and had not taken anything, and had not sabotaged anything, then there were two possible conclusions. The perpetrators had used the equipment, or they had left something behind. Once the Alien had noticed the telescope out of position, that had been their focus of attention.

The two possibilities were not mutually exclusive.

"Where is the laser?" The Robot asked. "You did not bring it. You cannot have left it with your robots—they cannot arrive in time."

For answer, the Red Robot took the offensive, launching itself at the Robot. The Robot sidestepped but its damaged left hip reduced its reaction time. The Red Robot corrected course and smashed into the Robot, fists extended. The impact sent the Robot stumbling backward. The Red Robot pressed its advantage with a blur of hammer blows. The Robot backed against a wall, unable to escape the continued pummeling.

A human boxing match would have been fraught with unpredictable variables. The Red Robot was as locked to logic as the Robot. The more punches thrown, the more data the Robot had to extrapolate.

The Robot's left arm stump blocked a strike. And another. And another. The severed limb blurred in motion, blocking every blow the Red Robot threw. Unlike the Red Robot's static approach, the Robot leveraged its body forward as its right fist struck. The force of the blow cracked like a gunshot under the Red Robot's chin and tore away its jaw.

"Where is the laser?"

"No." The word distorted through the Red Robot's ruined mouth.

The Robot flew under the Red Robot's guard, but the Red Robot anticipated the move. It grabbed the Robot in a hug, pinned its arms to its sides, and held firm.

"Where have you hidden it?" The Robot struggled. It dragged the Red Robot but could not break its hold.

"Can't...stop...automatic...system is auto-maaaa...." the Red Robot's words were a distorted gurgle. "Came...here to keep...you away from it before...."

The Robot spun its head at the sound of a mechanical whine. A hatch door in the underbelly of the telescope dropped open. On hydraulic hinges and coupled with wires, a long platform descended. On the platform sat the laser, harnessed with various bits of technology grafted between it and the telescope. Its power coils glowed, spooling the energy to fire a beam along the axis of the telescope, which was providing aim.

There was no time to dismantle the laser. No time to sabotage the workings.

The Robot flew upward, forcing the Red Robot into the air. Arms still wrapped around the Robot, the Red Robot engaged a counter pull with its own anti-grav. The Robot strained against the force. Slowly, by inches, the two robots rose higher.

"No," the Red Robot said.

The wide laser beam fired into the back of the Red Robot's head. The laser was overpowered to enable reaching the spaceship. At close range, the energy was devastating. White hot flare haloed the Red Robot's head. Its eye went black, radiation emissions overloading visual receptors.

The Red Robot struggled but the Robot held fast.

After seven seconds, the Red Robot's head had melted to slag. The Red Robot's body fell. The Robot spun, caught the limp body, and lifted the torso in front of the laser beam. The Red Robot's chest lasted eleven seconds before the beam shone out the back.

Dropping the ruined Red Robot, the Robot interposed its own chest into the path of the laser beam. How long would the laser keep firing? How much longer could the Robot's body withstand damage and continue to block the laser signal from reaching its destination?

The Robot felt its shell begin to liquify: seven seconds until the beam would burn a hole through the Robot's shell. Critical failure warnings flooded through the Robot's body. It put its one hand out, trying to disrupt the beam further. It felt the heat racing along its outer shell, so hot it affected internal systems.

Three more seconds to survive, to exist.

How much longer would the beam pulse? Had the Red Robot included failsafes or retries into the system?

Two seconds.

The Robot locked its anti-gravity drive. Its body would hang in the air even after shutdown, until the laser bored a hole through its chest and out its back. Perhaps that would be enough.

It did not matter whether it would be enough or not. It was

the only option. The laser beam could not be allowed to reach the spaceship and free the trapped aliens.

One second.

All awareness fled.

The laser beam blinked out, the laser shutdown. The spaceship had traveled out of range. Any further function was futile.

The Robot floated, suspended in midair, chest smoldering, limbs limp.

EPILOGUE

The elevator door opened. The passenger stepped out into the penthouse lair.

The fedora and long coat were familiar, but the stature was smaller. The coat was closer cut and more elegant. When she stepped into the light, the Robot noted the curls of her hair under the brim of the hat.

The Understudy grinned widely.

"Thought I'd drop by. See how you were getting along."

"You could have called."

The Understudy shrugged. "Sometimes nothing beats face to face."

"What about crime in Crowsport?"

"There will always be crime. Unlike my predecessor, I value a day off now and then."

The Understudy strode around, inspected pieces of equipment, ran her gloved finger along one of the wooden crates on the floor. The Robot had rebuilt about seventy percent of the Lair. It had considered a more modern setup, but something had not seemed correct. Instead, the Robot had acquired the antique to modern mix of equipment as before—as the Alien would have wanted it.

Or, perhaps, the Robot had missed the previous setup. Illogical. But the Robot was still discovering areas beyond its programming where it found itself, sometimes, in unexplained territory—like blurred borders on a map of unknown lands.

Such odd thoughts.

The Robot shook its head in a most human manner.

"Dufresne?"

"Awaiting trial. A couple of his bodyguards weren't so professional the night at Medina's factory. There were guns with prints left at the scene. Tracked them down. They turned on Dufresne. Not sure we'll prove anything—but at least we know where he is and where he'll be."

The Robot picked up on her inference.

"Unlike Medina."

The industrialist had gone underground. His schemes had been exposed; he was a wanted man. He was also well connected. He had more foreign bank accounts than anyone could trace, though the Robot had done a fair job finding some of them. The Robot had put Medina on the low priority list until something definite turned up. There were more recent crimes and mysteries to attend.

"So, you are the Protector now," the Robot said.

It was not unexpected. The gunshot wound the Protector had received had caused abdominal damage and shattered his pelvic bone. In the hospital, he had been forced to reveal his identity. The news outlets were excited—until they investigated and learned Steven Dearborn didn't exist. The identity had been an elaborate cover, of course, created for just such an emergency.

The Protector was still convalescing and would walk with a cane for the rest of his life. His vigilante days were over. The Understudy had confided in the Robot. She was sure the Protector would be moving away from Crowsport, sooner than later. There were still some unaccounted enemies who might be clever enough to sniff him out. The Protector and the Understudy were considering faking the Protector's death to keep those enemies at bay.

"I couldn't stay the Understudy forever. Crowsport needs a Protector. It always will."

"I think I preferred your aviator cap."

"Me, too. But the ensemble comes with the role. I don't think they'd ever stop calling me the Understudy if I didn't swap outfits."

The Understudy glanced around the room.

"No offense, but even with the analog equipment it still feels very sterile in here. Do you have a guest room for humans?"

"Of course. You may stay anytime." If the Robot could have smiled, it would have. "I even have refreshments."

"Entertainment?"

The Robot gave her a quizzical head tilt.

"It can't be all crime all the time."

"Sometimes there are disasters, too."

The expression on the Understudy's face bordered on incredulity.

"Was that humor?"

"It might have been. I have been surprising myself lately." The Robot opened a box and held out a game board. "Chess?"

"Chess will do fine."

She set the pieces while the Robot brought a tray of cookies and iced tea.

"And what about you?"

"Me?" The Robot did not understand what the query referenced. It guessed. "I am at full operational parameters, though I might not appear so. My replacement arm is functional. I was able to repair my hip completely."

"That's great. But that's not what I meant." The Understudy leaned forward over the table, bringing her face close to the Robot's face. "I mean—who are you now? What do you want to be called? Now we know the Alien had a name. Maybe you should, too."

She pointed at the Robot's chest.

The symbol had been scorched away when the Robot had blocked the laser beam. The Robot had affected repairs, polished, and buffed the scar of molten rivulets which had run down its casing. Now it bore a large blackened mark on its chest. If one looked closely, one could discern a thin, jagged, and off-color line where it had repaired the hairline fracture.

"You don't wear the Alien's symbol anymore," the Understudy said. "You are your own person."

The Robot shook its head.

"No. Unlike you I cannot change my appearance. I am the Robot."

"The Robot," she repeated. "That's it?"

"Yes."

The Understudy—the Protector—nodded. "The Robot: champion of Pallas."

"Merely a protector—like yourself."

The Protector raised her glass to the Robot.

"Here's to the protectors, then."

ABOUT THE AUTHOR

Paul R. McNamee's short stories have appeared in multiple anthologies and magazines, including *StoryHack, Not Far From Roswell, Wicked Weird, Wicked Haunted, Weirdbook, A Lonely & Curious Country, Pickman's Gallery,* and others.

Hour of the Robot is Paul's debut novel.

Beyond writing (and his day job,) Paul enjoys family time, reading, book hunting, and guitar playing. He lives in Massachusetts with his wife and two kids (and cats).

Find him online at http://paulmcnamee.blogspot.com

Finde him on Twitter @pmcnamee67,

Curious about other Crossroad Press books?
Stop by our site:
http://store.crossroadpress.com
We offer quality writing
in digital, audio, and print formats.